FO 920

FACE TO FACE

Also by Frances Usher

MAYBREAK

FACE
TO
FACE

Frances Usher

Loretto School

05880

First published in Great Britain 1991
by Methuen Children's Books Ltd
Published 1993 by Mammoth
an imprint of Reed Consumer Books Ltd,
Michelin House, 81 Fulham Road, London SW3 6RB
and Auckland, Melbourne, Singapore and Toronto

Reprinted 1993

Copyright © 1991 Frances Usher

The right of Frances Usher to be identified as author of
this work has been asserted by her in accordance with the
Copyright, Designs and Patents Act, 1988

ISBN 0 7497 1054 3

A CIP catalogue record for this title
is available from the British Library

Printed in Great Britain
by Cox & Wyman Ltd, Reading, Berkshire

This paperback is sold subject to the condition
that it shall not, by way of trade or otherwise,
be lent, resold, hired out, or otherwise circulated
without the publisher's prior consent in any form
of binding or cover other than that in which
it is published and without a similar condition
including this condition being imposed
on the subsequent purchaser.

Contents

For my sister Mary
with love

'When I was a child, I spake as a child, I understood as a child, I thought as a child: but when I became a man, I put away childish things.

For now we see through a glass, darkly: but then face to face.'

I Corinthians 13, verses 10-11

Chapter One

I didn't know what to do. I wanted to tell someone. I felt desperate to talk to someone.

One evening in April, I tried to tell Phil. We walked right round the walls for nearly an hour. But he wouldn't listen. He was too busy talking about his father.

'Honestly, Nick, I'm sure he's getting worse. You wouldn't think he could, would you?'

He was striding along in front of me on the narrow grass path, talking over his shoulder, hands deep in the pockets of his ankle-length tweed overcoat. He'd bought that coat the week before in a Help the Aged charity shop. It was a warm evening but he had the collar up and he wore his long blue knitted scarf. Phil liked to stand out from the crowd – unlike me.

'Don't you think he's getting worse, Nick?'

Why couldn't he listen to me for once? That's why I was out there, instead of getting on with my biology homework.

I said neutrally, 'Yes, probably.' It was best to be neutral when Phil started talking about his parents. He could change sides very suddenly. This time, obviously, it was his father's turn to be in the doghouse.

'He is, you know. Getting worse. He's driving Mum nuts. I mean, look what time he came home last night.'

We were just rounding the north-west corner of the walls and, without warning, he flopped down on a seat. I tripped over his outflung feet and collapsed beside him.

'Half-past one.' Phil said it with gloomy satisfaction. 'Half-past *one*. He woke me up, putting the car away. And the neighbours, probably.'

Phil's father was supposed to have some sort of girl friend in Bournemouth and another in Dorchester, and to be forever on the brink of moving in with one or other of them. I'd been quite disappointed the first time I'd met him; he didn't seem at all the raving Romeo I'd been expecting, just a quite friendly balding man no different from anyone else's father. But you could never tell, I suppose.

Someone had carved SARAH 4 MATTHEW into the wood of the seat. I ran my fingers over the letters. The carver hadn't managed the 'S' very well; it was a back-to-front 'Z'.

I said, 'Phil, listen a moment—'

'He hasn't got a clue about all the trouble he's causing. I'm the only one that sees it all.'

I sighed. It was hopeless.

Below us, the traffic was streaming along the bypass. I watched the train from Weymouth pulling into the station. Suddenly I longed to be on it, getting out of this town where I'd lived all my life, getting out of Dorset, going up to London or somewhere, just to escape.

I stood up. 'Come on, nearly half-past seven. I'm going home now.'

Would it help if I went away? Probably not, I thought. You can't run away from what's inside your head.

I don't know what sort of walls you've been picturing— something like Hadrian's Wall, perhaps, or the ones round York?

2

Our town walls aren't on that scale. They're just made of earth and covered with grass. People walk their dogs around them and use them as short cuts from one part of town to another. As you walk round, the view constantly changes.

No one knows who built them. They were certainly there in 1213, because that year a guy called Peter de Pomfret was dragged through the town tied to a horse's tail and hanged on the walls. The place where they hanged him is known today as 'Bloody Bank'. I cycle past it every day on the way to school and I often think of poor old Peter de P. What he'd done was to prophesy – wrongly as it turned out – that the king would not reign after Ascension Day. Nowadays, of course, he'd be interviewed on Breakfast TV and be given a slot doing horoscopes. He was just born in the wrong century.

The sun was low as we turned the last corner. Phil was still talking.

'Guess what Dad came out with this morning, Nick, just as I was leaving for school? He wants us to go to Florida in the summer holidays.'

'Lucky you.'

He snorted. 'It's his guilty conscience. Who wants to go to Florida? All that Disney rubbish.' He hunched his shoulders even tighter.

'I wouldn't mind,' I ventured. 'It'd be a good laugh.'

'You go, then.' He jumped down to the road. We'd gone as far as the walls could take us. This fourth side had the river to protect the town instead. I could see a cluster of white masts, seemingly growing out of the middle of the fields. They were the yachts that came up from Poole Harbour and moored at our Quay. They couldn't go upriver any further because of the low bridge.

'Let's get summer jobs, Nick. On one of the oil fields. Labouring or something. Earn lots of money.'

'Could do.' Generally in the summer I worked with Mum and Dad in the shop. 'Would they take us on at our ages?' I was nearly fifteen; Phil a bit older.

'Course they would. That's where the money is, my son. In them there hills.'

He nodded at the line of Purbeck Hills, dark against the evening sky. Oil's been found there in lots of places, and under the harbour and out at sea too.

We walked in silence towards the Quay. The graves in the churchyard were bright with daffodils and tulips. DEARLY BELOVED ... SADLY MISSED ... TILL WE MEET AGAIN ...

I could see I wasn't going to tell Phil after all. He'd never even noticed I'd been trying to. We'd known each other for years, right back to First School. We'd probably even played in the same sandpit, if I could remember that far back. And, always, Phil had done the talking and I'd done the listening. That's how it had always been. It wasn't going to change simply because, just for once, I very much needed to talk to someone.

After Phil had gone, I hung around the Quay for a while. The yachts and motor cruisers bobbed at anchor. People were strolling along the river bank and lounging outside the pub with a drink. I watched a pair of swans bringing their five fluffy cygnets under the bridge.

Suppose I had talked to Phil. Told him.

'*Dreams?*' he probably would have said. '*Is that all?* You think that's a problem? You wait till you have a home life like mine, mate. Then you'll know what problems are.'

True, of course. My family wasn't like his. I never

had to go round saying my parents didn't understand me. On the whole, I reckoned they understood me about as well as I understood them. Certainly we'd never gone in for serious rows, perhaps because Mum and Dad had always worked together running the shop; they'd had to get on.

But... 'Yes,' I could have said to Phil, 'I have dreams. And I can't bear them any longer.'

Does that sound wimpish? At one time, I would have thought so too. Dream what you like, as long as you keep it to yourself. That would have been my attitude. You dream yours and I'll dream mine.

But that was before these dreams began.

It was as if I had an enemy somewhere who had picked me out – just me – and who night after night was coming over to bombard me with dreams. Terrible dreams. Dreams like nothing I'd ever had before.

It had been going on for about six weeks, nearly every night. Every dream was the same. And, unlike most dreams, they stayed in my memory in every single detail.

I'm standing in these ... corridors. They stretch far into the distance, on and on. Everything is creamy-white. It's very quiet. The ground under my feet is thick and soft, and the air is thick and soft too.

I have to get out. Somewhere at the end of one of these corridors is safety. But I have to reach it. It's the only hope.

I start to run.

Almost at once, the corridor I'm in begins to twist. I find myself turning corners, corners that weren't there a moment before. As I hurry round each one I'm praying it will be the last, that I'll see the way out ahead of me.

Instead, there's another corner. And another. I have to keep running. My chest hurts.

Occasionally, there are steps under my feet, just two or three at a time; sometimes up, sometimes down. They catch at my feet and make me stumble.

I have to keep going ... I have to. But now there's something else.

The sides of the corridor are closing together.

I try to push them back with the palms of my hands but they're too strong for me. They keep coming. There isn't room for me to run any more. They're squeezing me, squeezing me. I can't breathe. I'll be pressed to death –

Someone's laughing.

Someone is laughing, and calling me. I don't hear the words, just the voice. But I know it's me they're calling. Someone's calling and teasing me and laughing.

They're behind me ... no, in front. Where? ... I have to find them.

No, I mustn't. That's dangerous. I have to get out.

But the voice is calling me. I must obey it.

Push the walls back ... Make enough space to keep running. Don't be trapped here –

The voice again, nearer. My hand, groping, touches a door. The voice is coming from inside that room.

I turn the handle and push open the door.

I can't get in. There's a long white cloth hanging in the doorway and it wraps itself round my arms, my struggling body.

Then the cloth parts, and I see the face.

There are white teeth laughing ... black eyes glinting. Black hair, long and shiny, falling over the forehead.

I see it; stare at it; then the cloth covers it again. And then I see it once more, bigger – a giant face – laughing and laughing at me –

6

No ... NO ...

I'm awake. Gasping for breath. Heart thumping in the dark.

A dream. Not real after all.

Another dream.

'Hello, Nick.'

I looked round. It was my brother, on his way home with Mum from Cubs.

'Look what I made tonight.' He held up some sort of chart. 'Great, eh? I've got to fill it in every day. What are you doing down here by yourself, Nick?'

'Thinking,' I said.

'Shall I stay and help you?'

'No thanks, Dan. I don't think so.'

'Oh.' He pushed up his metal-framed glasses. 'Well, I'll go and get my skateboard, then, and have a practice.'

'In and out of these parked cars?' said Mum. 'In and out of the river? Talk sense, Daniel. It's much too dark.'

'Oh, *Mum*.' He picked up a wooden lolly stick and began snapping it in pieces and dropping them into the water. 'Can't I?'

'No. Definitely no.' She looked at me over his fair head. 'Coming, Nick? Don't forget that homework.'

'There shouldn't be homework in the first week of term. We need adjustment time. A homework-free zone ...'

She nodded, not listening. She'd heard it all before.

'Don't be long.' She was looking at me rather carefully. 'You need a few early nights, I think.'

The swans hadn't been fooled. They hadn't even bent their necks to look at the scattering of floating

7

sticks. They paddled straight through them and on down the river.

I stood and watched Mum and Daniel walking up the street until they reached the side door of R.H. FORESTER: *Baker & Confectioner*. I saw Mum take her key from her bag.

I'd better go and get on with that biology, I thought.

Was Mum right about early nights? Perhaps. Perhaps the dreams would stop then, and the corridors would fade from my mind and I'd be left in peace. Probably that was all I needed.

It was just as well, that April evening, that I didn't know a time was soon coming when, far from wanting an early night, I would wish I need never sleep again.

Chapter Two

Nick Forester ... Nicholas Forester ... Nicholas J. Forester ...

I was practising signatures, just to pass the time till the end of the English lesson. It was better than sitting there doing nothing.

Nicholas John Forester ... No, too long. *N.J. Forester.* Better.

We'd been doing a timed essay that morning to go in our G.C.S.E. files. That meant silence and the teacher's eye on us. I'd finished mine sooner than anyone, which was probably a bad sign, though I seemed to have written quite a lot. I could see Phil doodling on his paper rather than writing anything, while Alison and Cathy at the next table were both scribbling like fiends. Alison kept glancing at her watch and groaning to herself.

I yawned, feeling my eyes dry and aching. I'd had another dream last night. This one had been worse, if anything; the face bigger, more menacing.

Whose face was it? What was it doing in my dreams?

I had no idea. It wasn't the face of anyone I knew. It had no right to be in my dreams, laughing at me, frightening me.

I picked up a pencil and found a page in my rough notebook. I tried to sketch the face I saw. But after a few minutes, I gave up in bafflement. The trouble was, I didn't even know if the person it belonged to was male or female, young or old. It was just a face, intensely *there*, but impossible to —

'*Nicholas Forester*. That's twice I've asked you to collect the essays. Do try to wake up, please.'

As I was collecting my stuff at the end of the afternoon, I remembered that Mum had asked me to meet Daniel out of school and take him to the dentist. I often had to do things like that because my parents were busy with the shop.

'Now, Dan, you've got your toothbrush, haven't you?' Mum had been snatching a quick cup of coffee and a sit-down while Dad coped with the early morning customers. 'Don't forget to clean your teeth before you leave school.'

'But be quick about it.' I handed Mum a piece of toast and fitted two more slices into the toaster. 'It's embarrassing standing outside with all the mothers and prams. Be the first one out, Dan, will you?'

I might as well have saved my breath, I reflected, as I stood at his school gates. Kids had come pouring out, the mothers and prams had all vanished one by one, and I'd been left alone. Even most of the teachers had driven away. What was Daniel up to?

There was a large car park in front of the building. I could see a little group of children there climbing on to a school bus, but that was all.

Cursing under my breath, I started wheeling my bike up the drive. It seemed a long time since I'd been a pupil there myself; funny how much smaller everything looked now.

I caught sight of three figures coming out of a side door. Yes, one of them was Dan all right; he was ambling along as if he had all the time in the world. I waved to him, pointing urgently at my watch, and saw him change direction.

The bus was coming down the drive. I pulled my bike in to the side to let it pass.

I heard the roar of its engine and felt its hot breath as it went by. I glanced up idly at the children in it. The two boys in the front seat were digging in a bag of sweets, their heads close together. The girl behind them was sucking a sweet too.

The girl in the –

It wasn't possible.

It couldn't have been. I must have been seeing things.

It couldn't have been.

'Hello, Nick. I forgot. Sorry.'

I stared down at Daniel. I couldn't make my brain work properly.

'Want one?' He had a bag of crisps in his hand, his jaws munching.

I was supposed to tell him to stop eating. I was supposed to be taking him to the dentist.

'Dan –' My voice was husky, odd.

'Don't worry. I've cleaned my teeth.' He took another crisp. His friends had gone off down the drive. 'Let's go. I like going to the dentist. It's brill.'

I cleared my throat. 'Dan, that bus. That one that's just gone out of the gates ...'

'What about it? I'll push your bike for you, shall I?'

Numbly, I let him take it. 'That bus. There was a girl on it.'

'There were lots of girls on it. And boys.'

'Yes, I know. But this particular girl –'

'What particular girl?' He crunched another crisp.

I reached out and took the bag from him and stuffed it in my pocket. 'You'll have to do your teeth again when we get to the dentist's. Listen.' I stood still and

11

gripped his shoulders. 'There was a girl in the second seat from the front. On this side of the bus as it went out. Who is she? What's her name?'

'I don't know.' He goggled at me. 'I don't know what you're talking about.'

'Oh, come on, Dan. She goes to your school, you must know her. She was in uniform like all the rest, she was sitting on her own, second seat back. A girl a bit older than you, about – oh, I don't know – ten, eleven maybe. You must know who she is.'

'I don't. Let me go. We're late. We'll miss the dentist.'

I stared at him, and I wanted to shake him till his teeth rattled.

'I've got to know who she is. I've got to.'

A girl with black shiny hair and dark eyes. A girl sitting on that bus, who turned and looked out of the window at me, and laughed.

A girl with the face that I saw in my dreams.

Chapter Three

'What do you think, Quincey?' I asked. 'Tell me, go on. You think I imagined it, don't you?'

Quincey lifted one eyelid and looked at me seriously for a moment, purring faintly. Then the eyelid drooped again and she buried her nose in her black fur.

'I didn't, you know.' I rubbed the soft base of her ear. 'I didn't imagine it. You weren't there, Quincey. I was, and I know what I saw.' But she was no longer listening. She'd fallen asleep again, curled up tightly on the end of my bed.

I reached across her and unlatched the window. It had been raining most of the day, but now there were patches of blue sky and the air was cool and fresh. My room was right at the top of the house and I could lean out and look down past the ragged patchwork of roof tiles that surrounded my dormer window to the street far below. I heard the cars swishing up and down the hill on the wet road, as I'd heard them all my life, and the sounds of voices and footsteps as people went about their shopping.

I hadn't imagined it. A week had passed since it had happened and the girl's face was as sharp and clear in my mind as ever. The bus had passed me and a girl had turned round and looked at me and, although I'd never seen her before, I'd recognised her. *I'd known her.* Her face was the face in my dreams. Her face laughed at me in the dreams. Hers was the face that terrified me.

That didn't make sense. It didn't make any sense at all.

But I'd seen what I'd seen.

I stared out of the window, trying to work it out. It had happened all right. I knew that. But what was I going to do about it?

Every day now for a week, I'd rushed over to Daniel's school at the end of the afternoon, hoping to see her again. But the bus must have been leaving particularly late on the afternoon I'd seen her, because I was never there in time again. Each day I arrived panting at the gates, only to find that the bus had already left. Just once I glimpsed it disappearing down the road, but that was the best I could do. My school just didn't come out in time. I could only stand at the gates, fuming, while the kids and the parents milled around me. Meanwhile, the bus was already heading out of town and carrying the girl with it.

If someone like Phil had been in my place, they'd probably have simply walked out of the last lesson of the day ten minutes early. But I didn't seem to have that sort of nerve.

And yet I knew I had to do something.

The dreams were coming now almost every night, leaving me shaken and sleepless. I just didn't understand what was going on. I'd tried and tried to think of an explanation for it all, but I couldn't.

So surely the explanation would have to come from her, from that black-haired girl who'd smiled so oddly at me as she went past in the bus. She'd have to tell me what it was all about. I'd have to find her somehow. But how?

'I'm just off, Nick, to my class.' Mum put her head round my door. 'All right? Dan's down in the sitting room watching *Neighbours*. He wants to stay up for a film that starts at nine, but he really mustn't. He ought to be in bed by then. Don't let him get round Dad, will you, darling?'

'I won't.' I stood up and stretched. 'Don't worry.'

She was studying computing at evening class, and aimed to bring the shop accounts up to date when she'd learned enough. She was good at things like that. I was more like Dad's side of the family, I thought, as I followed her down my stairs. Left to himself, Dad would still be happily muddling along in the same old way as his father and grandfather, who'd both owned the shop before him.

As we reached the first landing and went on down the next stairs, I caught my great-grandfather's eye looking at me quizzically. That was always happening.

He was sitting very upright on a chair on the pavement, surrounded by the rest of the Forester family of his day. You could tell when the photograph was taken, because there was bunting strung all over the buildings, and a banner over their heads said: VICTORY 1945. The picture had hung on our landing all my life. Next to my great-grandparents was their son – my grandfather – wearing his long white baker's apron, and in front of him, leaning back against his legs, was young Roger Forester, aged four, who became Dad. FORESTER & SON: *Best Homebaked Bread & Cakes*, read the inscription over the shop window. Grandfather was '& Son' at the time. Later, Dad was. I supposed I could be the next one if I wanted to be, but I wasn't very sure I did.

Down in the shop, Dad was emptying the window of the unsold cakes.

'Now, remember what I said, Nick, about Dan and that film,' said Mum. 'You know how he'll soft-soap Dad if he possibly can.'

'I'll remember.' I opened the shop door for her,

15

setting the CLOSED sign swinging. 'I'll be the hard man.'

'Well, someone has to be.' She smiled at Dad and me. 'See you later. 'Bye.'

I closed the door behind her.

'Anything for the grot box, Dad?' I asked.

The grot box was a sort of retirement home for unsold or damaged cakes. Our family always had first pick of them before they were thrown away. Dan and I often had a dip in it when we first came in from school.

'You can put in those iced fancies,' Dad said. 'The fruit cake's all right for tomorrow.' He started to pack it away carefully.

'I'll get the dustpan.'

I crawled round the inside of the empty windows, sweeping up the sugar and stray currants that had dropped off the buns.

'Have you started your homework yet, Nick?'

'Not yet.'

We carried out the glass shelves to the sink in the little back room, and began washing them.

'Don't leave it too late then, will you?'

'Plenty of time.'

'The G.C.S.E.'s going to be on you before you know it, son. This time next year—'

'I know.' I dried the last shelf and hung up the towel.

'If you get it done in good time, we could watch that film. Once Daniel's in bed.'

'Well—' I paused in the doorway. 'I sort of said to Phil I'd go round there later on.'

'Ah,' he said. 'Phil. Yes.'

I knew without ever having been told that he didn't much like Phil. I didn't know why; whether it was Phil himself he disapproved of or his family. He would have heard all the gossip about Phil's father, of course.

You hear everything when you've run a shop in a small town for generations.

Just once or twice lately, I'd caught myself wishing Dad was a bit more like Phil's father in some ways. Not running after other women, of course. It was hard to imagine Dad doing that. But I knew Phil's father didn't take all the interest in Phil that Dad took in me; he was far too busy living his own life and he left Phil to live his. Of course, Dad was much more reliable, but all the same...

'If you'd just cover the chocolate stands now, Nick, I'll start sweeping. Then why not see if you could put in a bit of work before we have supper, eh?'

As I began draping the white dustsheets over the displays of Mars Bars and Kit Kats, an idea suddenly came into my mind. I'd thought of a way of getting to see that girl at Daniel's school.

I'd do it, I decided. Tomorrow.

Chapter Four

'Hi, Phil ... Cathy.'

I trailed my foot along the ground and skidded to a stop. Streams of kids were walking and cycling up the hill towards school in the bright morning sun.

'Hello.' Cathy flicked back her long fair hair. 'Listen, Nick. I'm telling Phil he ought to come to one of our sessions. They're fantastic.' She raised her voice above the sound of the passing traffic. 'We talked to Richard the Third last time.'

I straightened up from my bike pushing. 'You talked to Richard the Third?'

'And Hitler. And John Lennon. You can talk to anyone you like. You just call them up, like on the phone.'

'Ah.' Light dawned. 'A ouija board, is that what you're talking about? You all sit round in a circle and get it to spell out messages, right?'

'We don't get it to,' Cathy corrected. 'It does it on its own. You have to go with the force ...'

I snorted. Phil said, 'I don't want to know about the past. Could I ask it about the future, about what's going to happen to me?'

I suddenly saw he was utterly serious. Was he thinking of asking about his father's plans?

Alison had been walking along with us in silence. 'It's wrong,' she said in a tight voice. 'I don't think you should meddle with things like that. You don't know what it might lead to.'

'Oh, come on, Alison. It's only a bit of fun.'

We were passing the part of the town walls called Bloody Bank as Cathy spoke and I wondered what Peter de Pomfret would have made of her ouija sessions. Presumably he'd have taken them a lot more seriously than I did. But, I suddenly thought, what about my dreams? Why did they keep repeating the same sequence over and over – the running down the corridors ... the voice ... the face? Couldn't they be sending me some sort of message? Some sort of warning? I shivered. I hadn't thought of that before.

School was coming into sight over the brow of the hill. The others had started an argument about seances and horoscopes. Abruptly, I swung into the saddle and wheeled round.

'See you later, chaps,' I said. 'Phil, cover for me for a bit, will you? I'll do the same for you one day.' Phil and I were in the same tutor group for registration.

They broke off their conversation, startled. 'Where..?'

'Just someone I want to see,' I said. 'Won't take long.'

'Ah ha.' Phil grinned at the others. 'Nick's got a girl friend, do you reckon?'

'Tell us about her, Nick ...' But I was already racing back down the hill with no time to spare.

With Phil covering up my absence, I could count on perhaps half an hour before I was missed at the first lesson. I didn't know what time the buses carrying pupils from outlying areas arrived each day at the girl's school, but with luck I'd be there when they did. And I could grab the girl as she got off and at least make an arrangement to meet her somewhere and question her about my dreams. It was worth a try, anyway.

19

I reached the school and was relieved to see plenty of children still milling round the gates. And – yes – there was a bus up near the school in the car park, and it looked as if the kids were just getting off it. Hastily I padlocked my bike to the railings and set off up the drive.

I'd have to hurry. Already, the first few figures were disappearing into the building, with a teacher on duty at the door to see them in.

I squinted. I still wasn't quite close enough to see properly. But none of the hurrying girls looked quite like her. Not that one ... no ... no ... I was almost sure she wasn't among them.

I reached the car park and stood there, hesitating, while the last few children from the bus went inside. I looked down the drive, but no other bus was coming; that seemed to be it for the day.

I came to a decision. I wasn't going tamely back to school after this. She must already be inside the building. If she was, I'd find her.

The teacher at the door never glanced at me. She was deep in conversation with two boys about a lost bag. I simply walked in with a crowd of kids, towering over them like Gulliver.

The smell of the place took me right back. It was polish and overheated training shoes and dust and dinners and just plain kids.

Once out of the teacher's sight, I dropped out of the crowd and leaned against the wall. It was worth checking the last few kids still arriving.

They were talking, laughing, arguing; one or two of them shoving each other a bit. None of them paid me the slightest attention as they went past, all heading for the locker rooms further along the passage. Boys on the right, I remembered, girls further along on the left.

If I spotted the girl I'd have to be quick. I couldn't follow her there.

I scanned the faces, searching for that thick glossy hair, that smile.

Fair hair, dark hair, the occasional red hair. Not one was the person I was seeking.

A bell shrilled. At once, like a shaken kaleidoscope, everyone shifted direction. The kids were hurrying away, vanishing into classrooms. Several teachers passed me, chivvying everyone along. Doors slammed. Eventually, quietness fell.

I pushed myself away from the wall and went back to the door. The teacher was pulling it shut from the outside, but I just had time to see that there were no buses in the car park and the drive was empty. Then the door slammed shut. The teacher hadn't seen me.

I stood still. There's a choice, I told myself.

One: Get out of here, collect your bike and belt back to school before you're in trouble. *Two* ...

Two: Now you've got this far, go and find the girl. She must be in the building somewhere. There may never be such a good chance again. Just walk past every classroom, looking for her.

There was a row of classrooms beyond the locker rooms. They all had big windows looking out on to the passage.

Have you ever walked past a line of classrooms and tried to scan the thirty faces inside each one, while still walking along quietly and steadily, pretending to be invisible? Don't try it. It's impossible.

I couldn't look and walk at the same time, that was the trouble. And the kids often weren't in neat rows; they were all over the place. I was forced to stand outside each window and stare in, trying to focus on every face in turn. Sometimes the children were

21

bunched round the teacher; sometimes they were milling about like sheep without a sheepdog. In one room half a dozen, for some reason, were crawling on the floor. It didn't surprise me to recognise Daniel as one of them. At least he didn't notice me.

I got a lot of funny looks. One of the teachers saw me and came halfway to the door as if to question me. I hurried on to the next window.

'This is ridiculous,' I thought. 'Creeping round like one of the Famous Five on a bad day. Better get out of here before you're thrown out.' I'd come to the last classroom anyway.

And I saw her.

There was no need to search at all. I saw her at once. She was not a metre from me, just on the other side of the glass. I couldn't see her face properly because she was turned away from me but there was no mistaking that thick shiny hair, shoulder length, cut in a fringe. And it wasn't only that; it was the way she was sitting. Somehow, I knew that was the way she'd sit in class. At the same table as other children, yes, but *apart* from them, separate. She was leaning on one elbow, and digging the point of a pencil into the table in front of her. She looked bored, distant; a bit sulky.

And then she turned her head. And my stomach gave a jump because she looked right at me and she was smiling, just as the face was always smiling in the dreams. A sly, knowing smile. Right at me.

I couldn't move, couldn't unlock my eyes. She knew something ... Everything. It was the dreams again, holding me helpless ...

'Are you looking for someone?'

I jumped out of my skin. I hadn't seen the teacher coming across the classroom, opening the door. A man with a beard, bushy eyebrows raised.

22

'Oh, it's Nicholas, isn't it? Nicholas Forester?' He'd always been good at people's names.

'Yes – um – Mr Scott.' What was I going to say? *Tell me that girl's name, please?* She'd turned away, seemingly uninterested. I couldn't see her face any more.

'Is it your brother you want? Daniel?'

'No, no, I –'

'You've gone past his class.' He was steering me back along the passage. 'Three doors back.'

'Right.' I tried to free myself. 'I'll be all right now.'

Too late. He was tapping on the door, taking me in. Faces were gaping at me.

'Daniel Forester's brother,' he said. 'Seems to be wandering about. Can you sort him out, do you think?' And to me, 'Nice to see you, Nick.' He was on his way out. 'Everything going well, is it?' He didn't wait for an answer. The door closed behind him.

'Daniel's brother?' This teacher must have come after my time at the school; she must be Mrs Reynolds, the class teacher Daniel was always talking about.

She was looking at me questioningly. I couldn't think of anything to say. I caught sight of Daniel, his face startled and red with embarrassment.

'Yes,' I said at last, breaking the long silence. 'But it's all right, thank you.'

I was backing towards the door, groping for the handle. Someone near Daniel giggled.

'Sorry,' I added. It was all I could think of to say.

There was trouble when I got back to school, of course. I rushed into maths very late, and had to apologise in front of everyone. I couldn't cope with the work properly because I'd missed all the explanation, and I knew I'd never manage the homework. Worse still, I had a message from my tutor that she wanted to see me at Break.

She wanted to know why I hadn't been at registration. Obviously, Phil hadn't covered up for me very well. Perhaps I should have asked someone else to do it. Anyway, it was an awkward few minutes.

It had been worth it, though. I sat through the rest of the day pondering on what I'd achieved:

First, I'd had another look at the girl, closer this time. If I'd ever had any doubt that she was the one in my dreams, that had completely gone now.

Secondly, I was sure now that somehow she held the key to the whole mystery. It was almost as if she'd been waiting for me to turn up. As if she'd known I'd come. She knew about me all right; she knew about my dreams. How she did, I had no idea, but I kept seeing that smile – a smile that said she knew something I didn't. I had to find out what it was.

One thing I'd learned that might be useful was which class she was in. That might help in tracking her down.

Because I was going to track her down. I was going to get this whole business sorted out. Why should I go through all that terror, all those sleepless nights, while a kid like that just sat and laughed at me?

I sat down in my room that evening with my maths books, but my heart wasn't in it. I kept seeing the girl's face as I'd last seen it in that classroom. She had quite a podgy, round face, and those black eyes had slid sideways to look at me through the hair that fell over her forehead. There was something – grubby – about her. Not that she was dirty or anything; it was just that there was a grubbiness somewhere. Inside.

In the end, I gave up the maths and went down to the

sitting room to watch TV.

'Homework all finished, Nick?' Dad asked.

'Mm.' I'd have to have another go at the maths the next day.

Daniel was kneeling at the coffee table, drawing pages of dinosaurs. 'Nick,' he began, 'this morning, why did you –'

'Sh.' I threw a warning glance at Mum and Dad, who were watching the News. I knew what he was going to ask.

He lowered his voice to a hissing whisper. 'You must have wanted me for something ...'

I shook my head.

'What did you come in for, then?'

'Dan, do you mind?' I got up and went to sit next to Mum. 'I'm trying to watch this.'

In fact, the News was rather horrible. There'd been a big train crash at evening rush hour and pictures of it filled the screen. Two trains had collided; lots of people had been killed and trapped in the wreckage. Shocked survivors with blood on their faces were being led away by rescue workers.

Later, in bed, I couldn't get it out of my head.

Suppose there'd been someone, somewhere, who'd known that crash was going to happen? Someone who could see into the future? They could have saved everyone.

Only people in certain carriages were killed. Others walked away uninjured. If someone had know it was going to happen, they could have rushed through the train at the last minute yelling: 'Out of here, quickly, quickly. Up the other end of the train ... Quickly ...'

Then there wouldn't have been any casualties. Everyone would have reached home safely that evening.

There are supposed to be people who can see the future like that. Peter de Pomfret must have been one of them. After all, he might have been wrong on his last prophecy and been hanged for it, but he must have been right most of the time or no one would have listened to him. How did he do it? Did he have visions? Or dreams?

The idea came back to me that my dreams were a warning of something that was going to happen. Perhaps I was being given a chance to save myself.

Suppose I found myself one day in those corridors — this time not in a dream but for real? I'd find out then what it was I was so scared of. But it would be too late to save myself.

And yet what good was a warning I didn't understand?

The girl knew what was going to happen. I really believed that. In some way I didn't understand, she'd be there when it did happen. But she wouldn't stop it. No — she'd be there laughing.

Restlessly, I turned over. I had to try to forget the dreams, forget the train crash, forget the girl. I had to try to go to sleep.

But don't let me dream, I thought. Please. Please. Just let me sleep.

Chapter Five

A few evenings later I went out to sit on Bloody Bank. From there I could look down at a little car park, empty at that time of day, where Daniel was skateboarding with his friends. I sat there and watched them twisting and leaping and occasionally falling.

After a time, Daniel's head appeared over the edge of the bank. He was dragging his skateboard behind him.

'Hello,' he said. 'Have you come to watch me? Did you see what I just did?'

'Yes, brilliant. Super mega brill. Dan –'

'Yes?'

'Listen. There's a girl at your school, in Mr Scott's class –'

'Girl?' He hadn't forgotten all the questions I'd asked him after the bus incident.

'I need to know her name.'

'Why?'

'I just do.' I described her as well as I could.

'She sits by the window on the passage side,' I ended, 'and I think she lives out in the country somewhere. Do you know her name?'

He shook his head. 'No idea,' he said. 'Look, this wheel's loose.'

'Find out,' I said. 'Please, Dan, will you? Find out for me.'

I didn't think he would. But the next evening I bumped

into him coming out of the bathroom. And, after he'd rambled on about a bruise he'd got in P.E. that morning, he suddenly said,

'Don't you want to know, then?'

'Know what?'

'That girl's name.'

'Oh.' My heart flicked like a salmon turning in the air. 'Right. Yes.'

'I've gone to a lot of trouble.' Clearly, I didn't sound grateful enough. 'I checked the whole of Mr Scott's class in assembly; I had to keep turning round and I got told off. Then I went along to their classroom and had another look. Then, to make sure, I went out to the car park after school and there she was, getting on a bus –'

'That's fine,' I said. 'Just get on with it, Dan.'

'I am getting on with it. Don't bully me.'

'*Dan*.' I took a step towards him. 'Her *name*. Just tell me her name.'

'You're bonkers.' He started down the stairs. It wasn't till he reached the bottom that he called over his shoulder,

'If you must know, her name's Helen.'

I leaned over the banisters. 'Dan, hang on a minute. Helen who?'

'What do you want to know for? Why don't you find someone your own age to pick on?'

'Dan ... Please.'

'Oh, all right,' he said crossly. 'Her name's Mallory. Okay? Helen Mallory.'

Helen Mallory. All next day, the name was in my head. At last I had a name to go with the face.

It sounded right. Familiar, almost, as if I had already known it. Helen Mallory was the person who had got into my dreams, the person who had been there before

I'd ever seen her on that bus. That was the name.

Helen Mallory.

Dear Helen Mallory, I wrote. *I expect you'll be surprised to have a letter from a complete stranger. However—*

I ripped the sheet off the pad and sent it spinning across the room to join the rest of my efforts in the bin. I wasn't a complete stranger. Look how she'd smiled at me. She already knew me in some way.

I started again.

Dear Helen, Please excuse me writing to you like this, but there's something about you I need to know. Have you ever—

Ever what?

Ever got yourself into my dreams? Ever been inside my head?

I sighed. This was becoming impossible.

It was Saturday afternoon, and I was trying my latest idea. Now I knew the girl's name, why not write to her? I could explain it all more easily in a letter than I could talking to her. It had seemed the obvious thing to do. I just hadn't reckoned on how hard it would actually be.

I looked at the envelope lying on my desk, already addressed: *Miss Helen Mallory, Class 6S,* plus the address of the school. Now I even had doubts about that.

Would she actually receive it? Suppose the school secretary or Mr Scott opened it instead? Or perhaps Mr Scott would give it to her, but stand over her while she read it? Or – worst scenario of all, perhaps – she might open it and read it out to all her friends ...

'Oh, come on.' I picked up my pen again. 'Try another one.'

*Dear Helen Mallory, I expect you'll think I'm crazy,
but I see your face every night in my dreams —*

Oh, *God*. I couldn't send that.

Impatiently, I swept the pad and pen and envelope
off my desk into the drawer. I'd had enough for the
time being.

As I ran down the stairs I caught my great-
grandfather's eye again, looking at me from the
photograph. I made a face at him and ran on down
another flight to the shop.

'Hi, Mum. Any tea around?'

'... or this one's £3.75. They're always popular.'
Mum made shushing movements at me and went on
showing boxes of chocolates to a customer.

I retreated to the room behind, and found a pot of
tea there, almost cold. I went and made a fresh one and
took it through, together with an extra mug.

'Ah, good, Nick,' Mum said when her customer had
gone. 'I hoped you might. Let's have a look in the grot
box, shall we?'

I fetched it and looked inside. 'It's good news, bad
news,' I reported. 'Good news — there's half a
chocolate eclair. Bad news — it's the bottom half.
Otherwise, there's a squashed custard tart, two
meringues someone seems to have jumped on ...'

'My fault,' Dad said, joining us. 'I dropped them on
the way to the window.' He gulped down some tea.
'Joyce, can you take over now while I run Daniel to
this party he's going to? Perhaps Nick'll give you a
hand.'

He went to the bottom of the stairs. 'You ready,
Daniel? Hurry up now.'

'Are you doing anything special this afternoon,
Nick?' Mum asked.

'Not really.'

She looked at me over the rim of her mug. 'You look tired,' she said.

Why didn't I tell her what I'd been doing upstairs? Why had I never told her about the dreams? For some reason I didn't understand, I'd never mentioned any of it to her or Dad. I just couldn't imagine doing that.

Dad and Daniel came through.

'Now, Dan.' Mum smoothed his hair. 'Have a good time, won't you? I'll come and collect you in the car this evening.'

He jiggled about, anxious to be gone. He was the sort of kid who always got invited to parties.

'What do you reckon his secret is?' I asked Mum after they'd left. 'What makes him so popular?'

She smiled, cautiously lifting the custard tart from the grot box and chewing thoughtfully.

'You have friends, too, Nick. Not quite as many as Dan, perhaps, but some good friends. Dan's different. He's always been very sociable. And it isn't only boys who like him. He tells me he'll be the only boy at this party and he loves the idea.' She shook her head. 'He can't wait to get there.'

The shop bell pinged. She laid her mug down. 'Most of the girls today will be older than him, apparently. They just seem to have taken a fancy to him.'

'Incredible,' I said. 'I wasn't a bit like that when I was nine.' Then it hit me.

I went out to the shop. 'Mum, you don't happen to know –' But she was already wrapping up bread rolls and was too busy to listen. A flurry of customers were crowding in through the door.

'Nick, could you help serve, please?'

'In a minute, Mum. Something important ...'

I dodged round the customers and hurried out into

31

the street. I stood on the edge of the pavement looking both ways.

We don't have a garage attached to the house because there's no room for one. So Dad and Daniel would have walked round to where the car was kept. I'm probably too late, I thought.

No, there they were, at the traffic lights. I began to run. The lights were still red, thank goodness.

They changed to amber just as I got there. I tapped on the car window. Daniel's head jerked round. I saw his lips move.

'Wind down your window.' Someone behind them was hooting.

'What is it, Nick?' Dad leaned across. 'Trouble with the shop?'

'No, I just want to ask Dan something.'

'Quick, then.' The car behind was trying to overtake, its driver glaring at us.

I said breathlessly, 'Helen Mallory, Dan. Is she going to be at this party?'

'I think so, yes. Why?' Then his face changed.

'Oh, no,' he said. 'Don't you dare. Don't you dare come and show me up in front of everyone like you did that day at school.'

Dad was moving off. Daniel put his face to the open window. 'I'll kill you if you do that, Nick.' His voice floated back to me.

So he would have to kill me, I thought. I propped my bike against the garden wall and contemplated the home-made banner stretched over the front door. HAPPY BIRTHDAY TANIA, it read. 11 TODAY.

It hadn't been easy to convince Mum it was a good idea for me to collect Daniel instead of her.

'But, Nick, it's starting to rain. And it's the other

32

side of town. I can easily pop over in the car while you and Dad clear up.'

'No, no. Don't worry. I'll cycle over and walk him back. The exercise'll do me good.'

'Well, don't go yet. You're much too early ...'

But I wanted to be early. Finally, she gave me the address and I set off. She was right about the weather; it was pouring by the time I got there.

'Hello.' I smiled at the woman who opened the door. 'I've come for my brother – Daniel Forester.'

'Oh ... Right.' She looked at me doubtfully. 'You're rather early, aren't you? Come in out of the rain, anyway.'

Objective One achieved. I stepped inside.

It was quite a small house. If Helen Mallory was there, there was no way I could miss her.

A huddle of girls sat at the top of the stairs. I peered up, trying to see if she was one of them.

'In here.' The woman pushed a door open.

Sound gushed out like a volcano in spate. 'One and two and THREE and clap ...'

I winced. But I was in the right room. Objective Two.

'Wonderful,' Tania's mother murmured in my ear. 'We had an all-in party service this year to run everything. Music, competitions, prizes ... Everything.'

'Great.'

The room was full of chanting, stamping girls, their hair tossing and flying. A man in a sparkling blue suit was intoning into a microphone: 'One and two and THREE and clap ...'

'Your brother's been right in the thick of it,' the woman was saying.

'Yes, he's like that.' I'd already seen Daniel bopping about in the middle of the girls.

Where was she? Objective Three was to find her. I started to fight my way round the edge of the room, looking at everyone. It was terribly hot.

'... two and THREE and clap and turn and STAMP –' A pain stabbed through my foot.

'Sorry,' someone called. 'Come and join in.'

Hands were dragging at me. 'No, thanks.' I shook myself free and struggled back to the woman in the doorway.

'Helen Mallory,' I shouted at her. 'Where's Helen Mallory?'

'Who? I thought it was Daniel you'd come for.'

'It is. I – I've a message for Helen.'

'Oh I see.' Suddenly the woman became brisker, as if glad of something to do at last. 'Right. Why didn't you say? She's here somewhere.'

She scanned the room. 'She must have gone up to the bathroom or something. I'll go and see.'

I followed her out, my heart thudding. The door closed on the noise.

'Now ... Helen.' The woman peered up the stairs. 'Ah, yes. Up there.'

I strained to see. The woman called, 'Helen. Just a moment, dear. There's a young man to see you.'

There was a stir among the girls at the top. A figure detached itself and began walking down. I saw black shoes and white socks, grey calf-length trousers and a red shirt with sleeves rolled up.

'Me?' She was smiling. 'You wanted to speak to me?'

I looked at her and I couldn't say a word.

I cleared my throat. 'He – Helen Mallory?'

She nodded.

34

'You're Helen Mallory?' It seemed the only thing to keep saying.

'Yes.' She glanced at the woman uncertainly. 'Why?'

I spun round. 'Where's Daniel?' I ran across the hall and pushed the door open. 'Daniel!'

'One and two and THREE and clap –'

'*Daniel* ...' I was throwing dancers aside in my frenzy to reach him. 'Come here. I want you.'

'What is it? Don't, Nick.' Dimly, I was aware of everyone staring as I pulled him across the hall. Behind us, the music sputtered to a stop.

'What's the matter? You're hurting me ...'

'Look! No, up there. That girl. Look at her. Who is she?'

'My dear boy –' the woman began.

'*Daniel, who is she?*'

He threw me one frightened glance and then stared up at her. At her curly brown hair. At her puzzled brown eyes as she shrank back behind the others.

'It's Helen Mallory,' he whispered. 'The one you asked me to find.'

I shook my head and my hands went slack on his shoulders. I turned away, suddenly feeling very tired.

'No, Dan,' I said. 'She may be Helen Mallory. But she's not the one I asked you to find. She's absolutely nothing like her.'

I think the party fizzled out after that.

I apologised to Tania's mother, of course, but she still looked as if she'd like to report me to the cruelty people. She wouldn't hear of Daniel walking home with me in the rain, and begged a lift for him with the first parents to arrive. As a matter of fact, it was the Mallorys. They said they lived out at Corfe Castle and would be happy to drop Dan off at the shop on their way. So he climbed into the car next to Helen, both of them giving me wary looks as they went, and I cycled home on my own in the rain.

As soon as I reached my room I went to my bin and tore all my attempted letters to Helen Mallory into tiny shreds. All I could think was: Thank goodness I hadn't actually sent her one of them.

Then I sat on my bed and stared blankly out of the window.

How could Daniel have done it? Picked out the wrong person like that? I'd been so sure ... It had just never occurred to me he could have made a mistake.

Now I was back at square one.

A man was walking down the hill from the newsagent's, struggling to keep his umbrella up with one hand while with the other he was trying to fold his evening newspaper so that he could read the front page. Two women crossed the street below me, their heads bent against the rain. I watched them until they were out of sight. Then my eyes came back to the pavement below me.

And the girl was there, just about to cross the street.

I knew her at once, although her back was to me. There could be no mistake.

She reached the opposite pavement. Then she turned round and looked up at my window. The hood of her jacket was up and her hands were thrust into her pockets. She looked soaking wet.

She looked steadily at me for a long moment. The same smile was on her face. Then she turned away and disappeared down a side street.

I scarcely felt my feet touch the stairs as I thundered down the two flights. I wrenched open the side door into the street and ran straight across, heedless of any cars coming down the hill. The rain lashed my face but

I didn't notice. I raced along the pavement and swerved into the side street.

Two boys were cycling into the distance. On the opposite side from me, an elderly couple walked along, huddled under a black umbrella. That was all. A wet Saturday evening had not tempted anyone else out of doors.

I ran along the street as far as the shopping centre and car park. There were still quite a number of cars there, although the shops were closed now. There was just a chance the girl could be there, waiting for her parents, perhaps. But although I searched until I was wet to the skin, there was no sign of her.

Chapter Six

I think it was after that that the situation began to slip out of my control, that I began not to care what I did so long as I found the girl. Began, perhaps, to lose my mind a little.

I've got to talk to her ... I must talk to her. The words pounded in my head each day as I cycled to school; as I sat, unhearing, unseeing, in class while lessons went on over my head; as I climbed wearily to my room to face another night of dreaming.

For the dreams hadn't stopped. If anything, they were worse. Once or twice I'd even woken from a dream, shaking and sweating as usual, calmed down a little, dozed off *and dreamed it all again*. It was as if there was a message in the dreams that I still wasn't receiving, and so they were being run through again and again.

I had to make them stop. They weren't going to stop on their own. Doing nothing wasn't going to get me anywhere. Doing nothing was unbearable.

I had to find that girl. I had to talk to her.

'Binoculars.' I said it aloud. 'That's what I need.'

I was prowling up and down the lane that ran along the back of Daniel's school. Every now and then I stopped and peered again through the mesh fence separating the lane from the school playing field. The air was full of shouting, screaming voices, and what seemed like thousands of children ran and leapt and played all over the field. How was I ever going to pick out the right one?

I wasn't meant to be there. On that particular day I was supposed to be at a lunchtime rehearsal for our end of term show. But the school drew me like a magnet. It was where I'd first seen the girl, and I couldn't keep away from it; I'd taken to going over there every day in my lunch hour. Even in the evenings at home and the weekends, I spent most of my time looking out of my bedroom window just in case I should see her again crossing the street, although I never did. She was beginning to haunt me.

Once again I stopped and looked through the wire fence. It was hopeless. I was never going to spot her like that.

That evening, I waited till Mum and Dad were settled in front of the television and then I tiptoed down my stairs to the cupboard on the landing. Yes, Dad's birdwatching binoculars were there, hanging in their case on the back door.

'Nick?' Dad had come out of the sitting room to go to the bathroom. 'Are you looking for something?'

I jumped guiltily.

'I thought you wouldn't mind if I borrowed these tomorrow,' I explained lamely. 'For something I'm doing at school.'

He frowned. 'As long as you don't lend them to young Phil or anyone,' he said. 'You've only got to ask, Nick. I know you'll be careful.'

'Thanks, Dad.' I wished he hadn't seen me. He knew as well as I did that I hadn't been going to ask his permission. I wished, too, that I could explain the real reason I needed them, to tell him all about the dreams and the corridors. But somehow I couldn't do that. There was something inside me stopping me. Sighing, I

39

went to put the binoculars in my school bag, ready for the morning.

And they made all the difference. Next day, back at Daniel's school, I stood close to the wire fence and made a sweep of the whole field, focusing on each group of children in turn.

Was that her, talking to a couple of boys near the path? No, too tall. What about that one, playing rounders with some other girls? No, no. She wasn't dark enough.

I moved on, fiddling to bring the figures into sharper focus. There were a few trees at the corner of the field. I moved on ... And back.

Someone was sitting under a tree. She wasn't reading, she wasn't doing anything at all. She was just sitting there alone, facing me.

My hands were shaking and I tried to steady them. Was it her?

'Playing I-Spy?' asked a voice behind me.

Phil, Cathy and two or three others were standing in the lane, eating chips and staring at me.

I shook my head and went on looking through the binoculars.

'What are you looking at, Nick?'

'A girl.' Her hair was hiding her face, that was the trouble. *Was* it her? 'Just a girl.'

There was a howl of laughter. 'A girl! What — here?'

'Nick fancies them young—'

'He's joined the dirty mac brigade,' said Phil. 'You want to be careful, Nick, creeping round the back of schools and looking at little kids through binoculars. You'll get yourself arrested.'

I felt my face grow hot and pushed the binoculars behind my back. 'I don't know what you mean.'

'Come and see me some time, Forester, and I'll explain it to you ...' They moved on, laughing and cat-calling.

Damn them. *Damn*. Slowly I wound the strap round the binoculars and slid them into their case. I started to follow the others back to school.

Phil turned round and saw me. 'Cheer up, mate,' he said, waiting for me. 'I won't sell your story to the *News of the World* – not this time.' He grinned, seeing me about to protest. Then he had one of his abrupt changes of mood.

'Hey, guess what, Nick? I've landed myself a job for the summer. It's at a place called the Coulson Arms, out in the country. Very up-market. I'll be a sort of assistant catering manager. Look.' He pulled a piece of paper from his pocket. 'I saw it in the Job Centre.'

I glanced at it. 'Oh, come on, Phil! Assistant catering manager? Some hope!' I began to read from the advertisement:

Job: Washer-up and Kitchen Assistant.
Details: Person required for mainly washing up of pots and pans, but also to help prepare lunchtime bar snacks, and to carry out other kitchen duties. Applicant must be able to fit into existing happy working team. Previous experience not necessary.
District: Coastal village, Purbeck.
Wage: To be arranged.
Hours: 9.30a.m. – 3.00p.m. 5 day week.
    Summer period only.
Age: Open.

'It's got loads of potential,' said Phil, pocketing the paper again. 'I expect I'll be taking over the cooking in a week or two.'

I laughed incredulously. 'Want a bet? You don't know a thing about cooking. I can't think how you talked them into taking you on.'

'Ah, well, they haven't actually taken me on yet,' he admitted. 'But they're sure to. I've got an interview tomorrow at five with the Big Cheese there – a guy called Briggs. He told me on the phone I'm the only one being interviewed, so the job's as good as mine, isn't it?' He held out his bag of chips. 'Want the last few? Go on, I'll let you.'

My stomach rumbled. I remembered I'd missed lunch yet again.

'Thanks.'

We walked on together. I hesitated. Then I said, 'Phil?'

'Yep?' He screwed up the chip bag.

'That binocular business just now. It wasn't what you thought. Honestly, it's nothing like that.'

'Oh?' He raised his eyebrows. 'What is it, then?'

I had to tell someone. I had to. As we strolled back to school, I began to talk. To tell him everything that had been happening to me.

I told him about the dreams. About the face I'd seen on the bus. About the girl in the classroom and in the street. About the Helen Mallory fiasco. And about my desperate, never-ending attempts to clear up the mystery.

He didn't say much. He simply let me talk on and on, while he mooched along with his hands deep in the pockets of his old overcoat, his eyes fixed on the ground.

We were very late for afternoon school, of course.

But what did that matter? I'd told somebody. I wasn't alone any longer.

'You'll keep it to yourself, Phil, won't you?' I asked as we went in. 'Promise?'

He looked at me with his light-coloured eyes, still distant even as they met mine. 'For these ears only, is it?' he asked. He did a mock military salute. 'Ja, ja, mein Kapitan. Over and out.'

I felt a weight had rolled off my mind. Whatever happened in the future, together Phil and I would be able to work out what to do.

That night, I went to bed for the first time for months without dread. I remember that as I drifted off to sleep, my last thought was that, for once, I'd be sure to sleep without dreaming.

But I was wrong. Quite wrong.

For that night, I dreamed again. And, this time, it was worse.

The voice was calling me. The cloth lifted. I saw the face. In my dream I screamed soundlessly.

Wake up ... I must wake up.

But I couldn't. I was running along the corridors, with no space to run. The walls were closing in. I had to force them back with my hands.

I rounded a corner. And another. And then –

My heart lifted. It was all right. There was a way out. *There* ... At the end of the corridor. It was going to be all right.

There was daylight at the end of the corridor. In just a moment I'd be out and everything would be all right. I felt myself laughing even as the tears of relief flowed down my face. I was going to be safe.

But – What was happening? Something was coming down over the patch of light – a panel, something like that – closing it off. I threw myself forward. I must reach it in time or I'd be trapped.

But even as I reached it, the panel slammed down. It was dark ... pitch dark. I hammered against the panel with my fists.

No, don't leave me here, don't shut me in ... Save me ... Let me out ... HEEELLLLLPPP –

I thrashed and fought, my heart slamming in my chest. It was dark. I couldn't breathe.

But it was my bedclothes I was fighting. I was in my bed. Of course.

Another dream. Yet another.

Why had the dreams suddenly got worse? It seemed wrong – unfair, almost. Now that I'd shared the worry of them with Phil, surely they ought to have got better.

I went to school next morning, grimly trying to force the dreams to the back of my mind. I felt heavy-eyed and stupid as I sat in class. I knew I had to make myself concentrate, or soon I'd be so hopelessly behind that I'd never catch up. Somehow I'd have to make up all the ground I'd lost. It could be done, I told myself. I just had to make it happen.

By the time I walked into lunch, I was feeling a bit better. The dreams – the girl – were not going to win. I was in charge of my life. I'd run it my way. And the first thing was to have a proper meal, not hang round Daniel's school.

But my new hopeful mood was not to last long.

Phil was in front of me in the queue, deep in conversation with a dinner lady. They were discussing the exact contents of a baked potato.

'Well, fancy meeting you here,' I said, pushing my tray along. 'Are you picking up some tips for your interview this evening?'

Phil handed back the baked potato and took some

44

sausages instead. 'I've changed my mind about the interview,' he said. 'I'm going to Florida this summer instead. I decided last night.' He picked up a raspberry yoghurt.

'Really? And what did the Big Cheese say when you told him you weren't going?'

'Not a lot,' he said. He put his tray down at the cash desk and dug out some money. 'Because I haven't told him. It's easier that way.'

I felt a spurt of irritation.

'Oh, charming. He'll be sitting there at five o'clock, waiting for you, and you won't turn up. Anyway, I thought you hated Florida –' But he'd already wandered off with his tray and I was talking to myself.

As I paid for my meal I saw Cathy waving to me from a corner table. I went over.

'Hi-de-hi, campers,' I said, putting down my tray.

'Hi, dream boy,' someone said.

A chill went down my spine.

I looked round the table. They were all looking at me.

'Had any good dreams lately, Nick?'

'Whose face did you see last night, Nick? Was it mine?'

'Oh, don't dream about her, Nick. Dream about me next time –'

'Is it true, Nick, you've got this thing about a ten-year-old girl and you dream about her every night?'

I couldn't speak. My mouth went dry. Phil had *told* them. When he'd promised me he wouldn't.

'Now, you lot, shut up,' Cathy said and pulled my arm. 'Sit down, Nick. I'm really interested in these dreams of yours. Do you ever –'

'Stop it.' My voice came out too high. 'Shut up, all of you.'

They stared at me.

I left my tray on the table and strode across the hall. Phil was sitting at a table on the far side, reading a doubled-back Asterix book as he ate.

'I want to talk to you,' I said.

He looked up. 'Oh, yes. Go on then.'

'You –' I choked on the word. My hands were clenched. 'Not in here. Get up. Come outside.'

'What are you so steamed up about?' But he got up and followed me to the big swing doors. He looked at me with concern.

'You've gone quite pale, Nick. You're not going to faint, are you?'

'Why should you care if I fainted? You don't care about anything. How could you do it?'

'Do it?' He frowned. 'Do what?'

'You know what. You know exactly what.' We both ducked as a crowd of people came in and the doors nearly hit us in the face. 'You've told everybody. The whole school ... About my dreams. About the girl.'

'Oh ...' He shrugged. 'That. Well, maybe I just mentioned it to Cathy. She's interested in weird stuff like that.'

'Weird ...'

'You know what I mean.'

I looked at him and I couldn't breathe.

'Oh, come on, Nick. Don't get hysterical. Let's go back and eat.'

'I don't want to eat,' I said. 'I don't want to see people. Everyone knows about it now. I can't bear it.'

'Oh, for goodness' sake – Look, I'm sorry if you're stewed up about this. But you'll have to see people. We've got physics this afternoon for a start.'

Phil and I were partners in a physics project. I'd have

to be with him all afternoon. I wouldn't do it ... I couldn't ...

Without another word I pushed past him and ran.

I'd almost got out of the building when I ran straight into my tutor.

'Ah, Nick, good,' she said. 'I've been wanting to have a word.' Then she looked at me closely. 'Are you all right?'

'Yes, thanks.' I turned my head away.

'Oh,' she said. 'Well, look, I've been thinking for some time you might like to come and have a chat about one or two things. What about now? I've got a few minutes.'

'Sorry.' I shook my head. 'There's some stuff I have to get ready for physics.'

'In a day or two, then?'

I nodded.

'You see, I've had several reports from other members of staff that things aren't going very well with you at the moment. I wondered if –' she hesitated – 'if there were any problems at home or anything like that.'

'Oh, no,' I said. 'Nothing like that. Everything's fine.'

'That's good,' she said, but she was still looking at me hard. 'As long as –'

'Yes,' I said. 'Thank you.' I smiled stiffly and walked off. I won't stay here another minute, I thought. I won't.

I walked out of the building and round to the bike sheds. Two minutes later I was cycling out of the school gates.

Chapter Seven

The grass along the sides of the country lane was long and thick, full of buttercups and clover and tall hedge parsley. An occasional car came past, but the drivers never glanced at me sitting there on the ground with my back against an old farm gate; there was nothing to disturb the peace but the sound of a distant tractor and the odd bee floating past my face.

I thought I might go on sitting there for the rest of my life.

There was no real reason for me to hide. I was several miles from school, well out into the country and, anyway, school must already have ended for the afternoon. If I was going to arrive home at anything like the normal time, I ought to get going. But I couldn't make myself do it.

There was such a heap of trouble piling up for me. First, I'd skipped school for the afternoon. I'd thought I wasn't the sort of person ever to do that, and yet I'd done it. Added to the number of times I'd been late back after lunch lately, I couldn't hope to get away with it.

Then there was my school work. I knew, too, that I was falling further and further behind with it. I'd had that one spurt of hope that morning, true, but now here I was missing lessons again. How was I ever to get on top of it? I was so tired all the time. And now I knew that teachers were beginning to notice and were talking to my tutor about me. I'd staved her off this time, but she'd corner me one day soon.

Worse than any of this, though, was the fact that all those people at school knew about my dreams and were gossiping and laughing about them. And like a heavy weight inside me was Phil. My best friend until now. I still couldn't believe he had let me down like that when I'd trusted him, when I'd needed someone to talk to so much.

I didn't know how to face any of it.

Slowly, I got to my feet. I'd have to go home. There wasn't anywhere else to go. I had to pick up my bike and—

Look out. Keep IN ...

I had no time to think. I simply heard an oncoming vehicle and flattened myself against the hedge as it whooshed by. I scarcely registered the words SCHOOL BUS on the front before I shut my eyes against the dust thrown up as it passed. Then I opened them and caught one glimpse of the figure on the back seat. It was the girl.

I wrenched the bike round and set off in pursuit. I'd done it before I had time to think, like a reflex action, like when the doctor taps your knee and your foot jerks forward. I didn't take in that I'd done it until I was half a mile along the lane, and by then I was pedalling so desperately I hadn't time to think about anything.

She was alone on the back seat, propped sideways in the corner with her feet up and her knees tucked under her chin. She seemed to be chewing. Her eyes were fixed on me, and the same amused look was on her face.

I hadn't known I could pedal like that. My hands were gripping the handlebars, the blood pounded in my head, my feet flew round and round.

Still smiling at me, the girl took a comb from her top pocket and began combing that black, glossy hair back from her face.

I was slipping behind. I had to keep going ... Keep going.

I guessed from the way the bus bounced along that it was nearly empty. It must have been dropping children off all along the way. Would I be able to keep up till it stopped again? How long would that be?

Faster ... I must keep up.

But I was losing ground. Steadily, the gap between the bus and me widened. I couldn't see the girl properly any longer.

Keep going ... Pedal harder.

At last, I caught sight of the bus indicator winking and saw it slow down. It was going to stop.

My face was throbbing with heat. I redoubled my efforts. Ahead of me, I saw someone stepping off the bus, jumping down into the lane. The bus began to pull away again.

It was all right. It wasn't her. It was a boy, already turning into a farm entrance as I passed him. Looking up at the bus, closer again now, I could see the girl still on the back seat, still looking at me over her shoulder, still chewing and smiling. I bent again to my pedalling.

We were going uphill. The driver changed gear once; again. I choked a little in the fumes. The hill had slowed down the bus, but it had slowed me too. I stood up in the saddle and forced the pedals round. I must stay on. If I had to get off and walk, I'd never catch up again.

Push ... gasp ... *push* ...

The bus reached the brow of the hill and vanished down the other side. I heard it accelerate away. Push ... Push ...

Then I was at the top too, and flying down the other side. The breeze was drying the sweat from my face. I'd catch up now ... I was going to do it —

CRACK. My front wheel struck something and the world spun round me. There was a burning pain. The bike was on top of me, its wheels still spinning, slower ... slower ...

And stop.

Then silence.

My hands were bleeding, my shoulder throbbing, my knees torn and scraped.

I sat there in the middle of the lane, not caring if a car should come down the hill and hit me because the bus was miles away by now and everything was ruined and finished.

I'd had enough. I'd had more than enough.

I let the hot stupid tears trickle down my face. Somewhere in the hedgerow near me a bird was singing its heart out.

I got to my feet in the end, of course. I brushed the gravel from my hands and knees as best I could and wrapped my hands in a couple of cleanish tissues. Then I picked up my bike, straightened the handlebars and discovered that it still worked, though the right pedal was a bit odd. I trudged back up the hill that, only a few minutes before, I'd flown down. At the top, I climbed on stiffly and began the long ride home.

I was going to be very late but it couldn't be helped. I'd think of something to tell Mum and Dad. Just at the moment, that wasn't important.

Something in my mind had cleared when I hit that pothole in the road and came off the bike. I hadn't just been shaken up physically; it was as if everything in my head had at last been shaken back into its right place, after months and months of wrong thinking.

I'd allowed myself to become obsessed by that girl. Look at how I'd behaved when that bus had come along. I'd set off on that crazy chase without any hope of catching her up, while she'd simply sat there, smiling.

There had been so much chasing round; so much damage done. My school work had gone to pot ... Mum and Dad were worried ... people at school were talking about me ... Phil ... I'd made a complete fool of myself.

It was as if a fever had gripped me. And now, suddenly, it had burnt itself out and gone. I was free.

If I ever saw that girl again, I swore to myself, I would ignore her. It wasn't too late to make a fresh start, to get my life together again. And if that meant that I'd have to put up with the dreams for the rest of my life – well, that was how it would have to be. Because I'd had enough. It was over.

I cycled past the farm where the boy had left the bus, feeling the ache in my shoulders and the smarting on my palms. I was so busy with my thoughts that I nearly missed the black and white signpost in the hedgerow, half-hidden by grass and flowers. It pointed down an even narrower lane to my right:

COULSON ARMS
HOTEL AND RESTAURANT
2 Miles
Accommodation.
Lunches, Dinner.
Bar Snacks.

So Phil's place was down there. I glanced at my watch. Quarter to five. The Big Cheese would be getting ready to interview him, not knowing he wasn't going to turn up.

Imagine passing up the chance of a job like that without even bothering to go for an interview. It probably wasn't a bad job; it could even be good fun. I wouldn't have minded it myself –

I drew a deep breath. Why not?

There'd been a phone box outside the farm, I remembered. I was back there in a minute and a half, fumbling in my pocket for change.

'Hello ... Dad. It's me ... Yes, fine, perfectly all right. I just had something on at school I forgot to mention ... Sorry, yes ... I know I should ... It'll go on a bit longer yet, I'm afraid ...'

It was terribly hot in the box. I pushed the door open with my back.

'Dad, listen. Someone's asked me round to his place afterwards to help him sort out some work. No, not Phil ... I don't think you've met this one ... Yes, yes, I will. Definitely by seven. I – Oh, sorry, my money's run out –'

I went out, picked up the bike and checked the time again. Ten and a half minutes to five. I had ten minutes to cycle two miles of hilly Dorset lanes, to find the Coulson Arms, to clean myself up and to present myself to the Big Cheese.

I didn't want to work with Mum and Dad this year and here was the chance. There'd be no more brooding over dreams and the girl. Probably the dreams would stop once I had something else to think about.

Just for a moment, I paused. Was I doing this simply to get back at Phil, taking his job away from under his nose? If I got it, he wouldn't be able to say he'd changed his mind back again – it'd be too late by then.

No, it wasn't that. It was all to do with making a fresh start. I'd seen that sign at exactly the right moment. It had been a sign for me – meant for me.

Chapter Eight

As I came down into the village, the church clock was striking a quarter past five.

I didn't have far to look for the Coulson Arms. It stood next to the little squat-towered church at the top of the main street, looking out over the straggle of thatched cottages with their gardens full of flowers and their 'Cream Teas' signs, to the sea half a mile away where the road ended.

Everything was very quiet in the late afternoon sun. I found myself almost tiptoeing as I wheeled my bicycle up to the front door. REAL ALES and GOOD FOOD said the notices; but the very solid-looking door was locked. I went over to one of the front windows and looked in, screening my eyes from the sun. All the stools and chairs were empty; there was nobody behind the bar. I would have to find another way in.

There was a narrow path between the side of the building and the churchyard and I began to walk along it. I realised almost at once that the Coulson Arms was much bigger than I'd first thought, and much older. The part that faced the village must have been modernised recently. Behind, the grey Purbeck stone walls were weathered and lichen-covered, and they ran back much further than you ever could have guessed. Eventually, I turned the corner at the end. Then I stood still.

I was standing at the edge of a sun terrace. There

were tubs of flowers, and a white garden table and one or two chairs, but nobody was around. It seemed I had come to a private part of the hotel. The terrace was edged by a low stone wall; three steps led down to lawns and a rock garden.

Standing guard over the steps was a lion. Its paws were planted foursquare on top of the wall. I hesitated for a moment. Then I crossed over to it.

It had a shaggy stone mane, and its back dipped like a saddle.

I looked at it. Slowly, I put out a hand to touch its head. Then I withdrew it again.

'Hey ... you!'

I jumped round. The voice had come from above me.

'What the devil do you think you're up to?'

A man was leaning out of a window above the terrace, a man with brushed-back grey hair and a moustache.

'You're not a guest here.'

I went a bit closer. 'No, I've come for an interview. For the job in the kitchen.'

'Interview?' He looked at his watch. 'Do you know the time? I thought we agreed on the telephone that you'd come at five.'

So this was the Big Cheese. 'Yes, I know. I'm sorry I'm late. I –'

'Wait there.' He slammed the window shut.

I went on standing by the stone lion. I didn't try to touch it again. Instead I fished out my rolled-up school tie from my pocket, and put it on.

The man appeared round the far corner of the building.

'Reception's round this side,' he said, turning on his heel. 'I can't think how you could have missed it.'

'I came round the other way.' I was hurrying to catch him up.

'Hm.'

We came to a door with a striped sunblind over it and I followed him in. There was lots of white paint everywhere, thick carpets under my feet, a bowl of blue and white flowers on a desk in the corner.

The man was looking me up and down, frowning.

'So you're Philip Dayton. Is this how you usually dress for an interview?'

For a second, I was tempted to let the name go. But I knew it wouldn't work.

'Actually my name's Nicholas Forester. Philip couldn't take the job after all and –' I launched into a confused explanation. 'But I want it,' I finished. 'If you think I'm suitable. I'd like it very much.' I was surprised how much I did want it suddenly.

'So you turn up here late, looking like that,' observed the man. 'Hardly a good start.'

'I came off my bike.' I was horribly aware of the torn knees of my trousers. 'I was hurrying and I didn't see this pothole.'

'There seem to be rather a lot of things you don't see. Not very wide awake, are you?'

'I am usually,' I retorted, stung. 'It's just today. Normally I am.'

He gazed at me for a moment, his grey eyes unreadable. Then he gave me a push towards a door labelled GENTLEMEN.

'Five minutes,' he said. 'Five minutes to smarten up and get yourself across to my office over there. All right?'

'Yes,' I said. 'Thank you.'

'And no longer,' he said. 'Or you'll find there won't be any interview.'

I was soaping my hands tentatively and watching the threads of blood curl away in the water when there was a tap at the door.

'Hello.' A fair-haired girl of about twenty put her head round the door. 'Is it safe to come in?'

'Sure, there's nobody here but me.'

'Mr Briggs asked me to bring you this.' She held out a first-aid kit. 'He thought you might need it.'

'Well, yes.' I couldn't keep the surprise out of my voice. 'Thanks a lot.'

'Here, I'll do that for you.' She unwrapped a couple of plasters and peeled off the backings for me. 'He's all right, you know. Underneath.'

'Oh, good. I just haven't done very brilliantly so far – falling off my bike and everything.' I tried not to wince as I patted my palms dry on a paper towel.

'He won't let you get away with a thing,' she said. 'But he's all right when you get to know him.'

I was trying to sponge the mud off my trousers. I couldn't do much about the torn part. 'What do you do here?' I asked.

'I'm the hotel receptionist. My name's Kirsty.'

'I'm Nick.'

I combed my hair and looked at myself doubtfully in the mirror. 'That'll have to do.'

'You look fine.' She pushed the door open. 'Go in and see him now. Good luck. I'll keep my fingers crossed for you.'

'Thanks.'

She gave me a smile and disappeared through a swing door. I crossed the hall to the door marked *Private*, hesitated a moment, then knocked.

Quincey was up in our old apple tree when I reached home. I saw her sprawling up there with her paws

58

hanging down on each side of the gnarled branch as I manoeuvred my bike through the gate into our back yard.

'Hi, Quince.' I couldn't seem to stop grinning. 'Caught any good mice lately? Oh, hello, Dad.'

He was standing on a step ladder, watering one of the hanging baskets. He turned round.

'You're back then, Nick.'

I wheeled my bike into the shed. 'Yes. Just made it by seven, like we said.'

I saw the little table had been set out in the last patch of sun, laid with three places. It was Daniel's choir practice night.

'Are we eating out here? Good.' I sat down. I could hear Mum rattling dishes in the kitchen.

Dad climbed down. 'What's been happening to you, Nick?' He looked at my torn trousers, my plastered hands.

'I had an accident,' I said. 'I came off my bike.'

'What? Where? Are you all right? You weren't hurt, Nick, were you?'

'No, honestly. Don't worry, Dad. It was nothing. Look, I've been nicely patched up.'

I reached for the crusty loaf and began trying to cut slices from it. One thing about our line of business was that we always had first choice of bread. But my hands were clumsy and awkward.

'Leave that a moment, Nick,' Dad said. He came and sat opposite me. 'I want to talk to you.'

I laid down the knife. 'Yes?'

'You weren't in school this afternoon,' he said. 'You were cycling round somewhere out in the country on your own when you should have been at school.' His eyes looked steadily into mine.

'How – how do you know that?'

'One of the customers mentioned it to me. She passed you in her car.'

Customers. You couldn't do a thing without someone seeing you and passing it on.

'And yet you phoned me,' Dad went on, 'and spoke as if you were still in school. You couldn't have been, Nick, when you made that call. And I don't think you went on to anyone's house afterwards to do homework, did you?'

When I didn't answer, he said again,

'Did you, Nick?'

I crumbled some bread into pellets. 'I didn't say it was *home*work. I didn't say anything that wasn't true.'

'Oh, not in so many words, maybe. But you meant to mislead us, Nick. And this isn't the first time you've missed lessons, or been late for them, is it?'

How did he hear these things? I bent down to stroke Quincey, who'd come over to rub round my legs.

'Now, come on, Nick. Tell me the truth.'

For a second, I thought I might – tell him the whole truth, about the dreams and the girl and everything. But, again, something inside me warned me that wouldn't be a good idea.

'Well ...' I said, 'I have missed lessons once or twice lately, I suppose. But there's always been a reason for it. Today, for instance, Phil and I had this row about something, you see, at lunchtime. I didn't want to work with him after that so I ... went away.'

'But Nick –' Dad looked anxious. 'You can't just take off like that when you're upset. You've got exams coming up next year for one thing ...'

'Dad, listen. Don't worry about my work. I know I haven't been doing very well lately, but I've decided. Things are going to change, I promise. I'm going to work hard from now on, get better marks and –' I drew a deep breath – 'I've got something else to tell you. I've got a job. For the holidays.'

'Well, yes,' said Dad. 'You'll work with us in the shop as usual. Won't you?'

'Not this year, Dad. I've been offered another job. It's really great. I'll be earning –'

'We always pay you.'

'Yes, I know you do. But –' How could I explain? For some reason, that stone lion came back into my mind as I'd last seen it when I fetched my bike from Mr Briggs's garden after the interview. I saw again the Coulson Arms at the top of the village street with the sea in the distance. There was something about the place ...

I described my interview to Dad.

'Mr Briggs didn't quite commit himself today, because he wants references and things, and there's a form for you to give permission because I'm only fifteen. But I'm sure he's going to give me the job. And it isn't just washing dishes; I might be able to help with the food later on. And, anyway, washing dishes'll be good fun –'

'Good gracious, Nick.' Mum leaned over my shoulder and put a bowl of salad on the table. 'Did I hear right? What are you talking about?'

'The boy seems to have got himself a summer job, Joyce,' Dad said. 'He says he doesn't want to work with us this year.'

'Oh, Dad. I didn't say I didn't want to.'

'Well, let's eat. And you can tell us about it.'

I painted as glowing a picture of my interview as I could and by the end of the meal I could see they were coming round to the idea.

'I'll look forward to some help in the kitchen after you've had a summer there, Nick,' Mum said. 'That will be a nice change.' Her eyes were amused.

'Look, there's this form to be filled in.' I pushed the dishes aside and spread it on the table.

Dad took out his reading glasses. 'You'll have to stick it if you go there, Nick,' he said. 'There mustn't be any running off if you don't like something. They won't stand any messing about.'

'I know. I shan't want to.'

'Now. *Name ... Address ... Date of Birth ... Hours to be worked* – You'll have to fill that in, Nick ... *Name of Establishment* ... What's this place called?'

'The Coulson Arms,' I said.

'What?'

'The Coulson Arms,' I repeated. I turned to Mum. 'You ought to see it, Mum. There's a fantastic view from the front, right down to the sea. You and Dad must come out one day and have a drink.'

'A drink?' Mum stared at me. 'Have a drink?'

What had I said wrong? 'Why not? Just to see the place. You don't have to get raving drunk or anything. I expect they do coffee or something.'

Mum didn't answer. I looked at Dad. He was staring down at the form. I noticed how grey his hair was becoming lately.

'What's wrong?' I said. 'I don't understand. I told you it was a pub as well as a hotel. Don't worry, I won't be allowed behind the bar. Mr Briggs is terribly strict about that. He told me. No one under eighteen's allowed near it.'

There was silence.

Mum said at last, 'I don't think I want you working in a pub, Nick. I hadn't quite realised what this job was. There's far too much drinking by young people going on already. If you want a job, there's a perfectly good one here for you. Where would working in a pub get you? What sort of work experience is that?'

'Oh, Mum! Why are you suddenly saying all this? It's too late now. Mr Briggs is –'

'I don't want to hear, Nick.' She pushed back her chair. 'You must talk to your father about it.'

She picked up a pile of dishes and went into the house with them.

I looked at Dad helplessly. 'I'm sorry. I didn't mean to upset her.'

'It's all right, Nick. It's not your fault.' Dad got up and went into the kitchen. After a minute or two, I followed him in, not knowing what else to do.

My mother was standing at the cooker, stirring something.

'He's growing up, Joyce,' my father was saying. 'You can't protect him for ever.'

'I know,' she said. 'I know that.'

I went and put my arms round her from behind. Already, I was half a head taller than she was. 'It'll be all right, Mum,' I said. 'Really. I won't be near any drink; I'll be slaving over a hot sink all day. Think how good that's going to be for my character.'

After a moment, she twisted round and gave me a watery smile.

'If it's really what you want, Nick. I'll miss you in the shop this year, though.'

'No, no,' Dad said. 'It's time for a change. I expect we can find someone else to help us. The main thing is for Nick to be happy. You'll be all right there, won't you, Nick?'

'Of course I will,' I said. 'Like I said, it'll be good fun.'

Chapter Nine

And so I came to the Coulson Arms.

Right from the beginning I felt at home. I stood all day at the big sink in the corner of the kitchen, an apron covering my T-shirt and jeans, up to my elbows in steaming soapy water, while the voices shouted and called around me:

'Hurry, Nick, I need those pans now ...'

'Three more chicken curries please, Chef ...'

'One rare sirloin steak, two medium ...'

'That Dorset Apple Cake's with cream, Mrs Baldwin, not ice cream ...'

'Nick, we're out of plates. Do me a dozen quickly ... quickly ... quickly ... quickly ...'

From first thing in the morning — when I was faced with huge pans sticky with breakfast porridge — all through the day, as plates coated with gravy or custard went through my hands one after the other, to the last back-breaking half hour in the afternoon as Mrs Baldwin and I washed the kitchen floor together, life for me at the Coulson Arms passed by in an exhausted blur.

'Here's the next load of cutlery, Nick. I'll tip it in ...'

'Empty the bin, Nick, will you? It's overflowing ...'

'Leave that now, Nick. Give me a hand with this ...'

My arms ached, my legs ached, my head ached. The hot water turned the skin of my fingers grey and puckered. I used to go home each day and collapse on my bed and swear that never, never again would I take a job in a hotel kitchen.

And then, about halfway through the third week, I made a discovery.

I loved it.

For the first time for ages, I was happy.

We sat on a bench outside the kitchen door, four of us in the sun, having our coffee break. Jeff, one of the young barmen, was suggesting ways of brightening up our toast.

'What about marmalade with peanut butter on top?' His eyes were half closed against the dazzling light. Below us, the village dozed in the heat. 'Or should you put the marmalade on top? Yes, that'd be better. Or Bovril and honey? That's quite nice ...'

Next to me, Mrs Baldwin shuddered to herself and took another sip from her mug.

'Or strawberry jam with ...'

In fact, plain toast and butter was what we always had, left over from the guests' breakfast. No doubt it was crisp and fresh when they saw it; by mid-morning, when it reached us, it was flabby enough to fold in half.

'Now, young Nick.' Mrs Baldwin heaved herself to her feet. 'We've had our ten minutes. Time to get on. Besides –' she lowered her voice – 'I can see the boss in there talking with Chef. Let's have your mugs, Jeff ... Kirsty.'

Kirsty, the receptionist I'd met at my interview, looked up from her quiet conversation with Jeff and smiled at me as she handed me her mug.

'See you the usual time, Nick. Don't be late.'

'I won't. Thanks.'

After a few days of cycling the long miles between home and the Coulson Arms, I'd been only too glad to accept Kirsty's offer of a daily lift. She and Beryl, one of the chambermaids, passed my house each day on their way to work.

I lingered a moment before returning to the hot kitchen, to breath in the warm scented air and see the sea shimmering behind the village roofs. Then I picked up the tray and followed Mrs Baldwin inside, leaving Kirsty and Jeff talking together on the bench.

Mrs Baldwin was slicing cucumbers at the big table. My draining board was stacked with dirty dishes. I began to refill the sink with fresh hot water. On the other side of the room, Mr Briggs was deep in conversation with Chef.

If I was at the bottom of the staff hierarchy at the Coulson Arms, Chef was at the top. He was a lean, dark man in white, who worked all day silently on his own side of the kitchen. My only contact with him was the steady stream of used pans that he handed me for washing; generally they came back again in a few minutes, used again.

Mrs Baldwin was friendlier. Her job was to do the vegetables and the bar snacks. I'd watch enviously as her hands flew over the dishes, turning out immaculate Prawn Cocktails and Stilton Ploughman's ready to go out to the customers in the bars.

'Now, Nicholas –'

I jumped. I hadn't heard Mr Briggs coming over.

'Is that water really hot?' He dipped in a hand. 'Hm.' He picked up one or two washed plates and ran a finger round them.

'Settling in?' he asked abruptly.

'Yes. Yes, thank you.'

He nodded. 'Well, you seem to have it under control now. Better than your first week, anyway.'

'Er ... Yes.' He didn't miss much.

He turned to go. 'Mrs Baldwin, you might be able to use a little help with the food now and then. When the washing up's all up to date, of course. Do you think?'

'I'm sure I could,' she said.

'Good.' And he was gone.

So promotion of a kind had come to me. I glowed for the rest of the day. Life wasn't all kitchen sinks.

As Kirsty had told me, Mr Briggs was all right when you got to know him.

'I made seventeen Prawn Cocktails in eight minutes today,' I said. 'Well, Mrs Baldwin and I did between us. We had this coach party in, you see, and we had to do everything at once—'

'Nick,' Mum said. 'I want to get cleared up quickly. Haven't you finished yet?'

'Nearly.' I took another mouthful. 'And then there was nobody free to take them out, you see, so they made me tidy myself up and do it. I had to wander all round the lounge with this huge tray shouting *Seventeen Prawn Cocktails ... Seventeen Prawn Cocktails*'. I felt an utter wally. Then I found the right customers but I got all muddled up between the people having white bread and butter and the people having brown—'

'Nick—'

'And then they all decided to have chocolate nut sundaes to follow and—'

'I wish we had stuff like that,' Daniel said longingly. 'Why don't you bring a few sundaes home with you one day?'

'What, and lose my job? I should — Hey, Mum, don't! I haven't finished.'

'I told you,' she said. 'I want to get cleared up. You'd

have finished by now if you hadn't talked so much. Of course, I expect you find my food pretty dull after all the fancy things you're used to now ...'

'What?' Bewildered, I looked at the plate she'd taken from me. 'But – This is from the takeaway, isn't it? You didn't cook it.'

'Of course I didn't cook it.' Her face flushed. 'If you think I have time to do Prawn Cocktails and things when I have the shop to see to from morning to night –'

'I don't. I didn't mean – I *like* takeaway food.'

'Your mother's a fine cook.' Dad tried to smooth things over and made them worse. 'When she has the time.'

'I never do have the time. Not now.'

Silently, Dad took the plates from her and went out to the kitchen. There was an awkward pause.

'Well –' Mum cleared her throat. 'What's everyone doing tonight?'

'I think I'll go swimming,' I said. 'It's so hot and sticky.'

'All right. But you'd better give Granny a ring first. You know she's expecting you and Daniel to stay with her in Plymouth at the end of August. You still haven't said if you're going or not.'

'I can't, Mum. My job was for the whole school holiday. We're just coming to the busiest time.'

She shrugged. 'All right, all right. But you must tell Granny. I know she's my mother but I'm not doing that for you.'

'I'll do it, don't worry.'

When she'd gone, I raised my eyebrows at Daniel.

'What on earth's got into Mum lately? Do you know?'

'I don't know,' said Daniel. 'She's always cross now. Ever since you started your job.'

Was she? Certainly, there seemed a lot of tension in the family lately.

I reckon my parents understand me about as well as I understand them. My thoughts went back to that April evening when I'd walked round the walls with Phil. That's what I'd said then. But it seemed very far off now. I wondered if it were still true. I didn't seem to understand them at all at present.

Most parents would be pleased to have a son working so hard in his holidays, earning his own money, standing on his own feet.

But mine simply didn't want to know. They'd never taken up my suggestion of coming out to the Coulson Arms; they'd never been near the place. They never asked how I was getting on, never showed any interest at all.

Why?

It must be because I'd found the job myself, without consulting them. And because I hadn't wanted to work with them in the shop this time. I remembered the family photograph: Forester & Son ... & Son ... & Son ... That's what they wanted. To tie me to the family apron strings for the rest of my life.

No way, I thought. No way.

I was happy at the Coulson Arms. I was going to work there all through the holidays, rather than going to Granny's with Daniel. Perhaps Mr Briggs would ask me to go and work for him again at Christmas. Maybe he would even offer me a permanent job eventually ...

The only shadow over it all was my broken friendship with Phil. Since the day of my interview, we'd scarcely spoken. He resented the fact I'd taken his job, as he saw it, while I still hadn't forgiven him for telling people about my dreams when he'd promised not to. At school, we avoided each other as much as possible. School work had taken up most of my time, anyway, but I'd still missed him a lot more than I cared to admit.

But I did enjoy the Coulson Arms. While I was there, I could forget about the dreams. They were still coming nearly every night, but they were no worse and I was, almost, beginning to learn to live with them.

As for the girl, I never saw her now. Since term ended I'd felt free of her, safe. Our paths weren't likely to cross in the holidays. She was probably even now at home somewhere, remembering me as she'd last seen me – falling from my bike into the road. Remembering and laughing.

Strange to think I still didn't know her name ...

'Dad's washing up,' I said to Daniel. 'Shall we go and take over?'

He made a face.

'Come on,' I said. 'I'm a professional now, remember. I'll show you how to do a High Speed Techno Wash. Then ask Mum if you can come swimming with me. We'll need to cool off after that.'

There's nothing like swimming, is there, for rinsing away all your tensions? I remember walking home from the Sports Centre that evening with Daniel, feeling my whole body relaxed and ready for sleep. And yet, that was the night I dreamed again. *And that time was the worst of all.*

It began the same as ever. The corridors. The voice, laughing. There was the usual confusion in my mind, the feeling of being pulled two ways. I wanted to go running to the owner of the voice, and at the same time I wanted to run away. And as usual the voice was too strong for me. I had to obey ...

I push the door open. And the face is there behind

the cloth. It's hidden; then it's there once more, huge and laughing. Black hair, laughing white teeth. I run.

To my relief, I catch sight of a way out at the end of the corridor. It's all as if for the first time. Joy floods into me. I'm going to be safe.

I race towards the light. But the panel starts to come down. I'll be trapped.

No ... I must get out. This time I WILL get out.

I hurl myself forward. I've never, never run like this. I'm going to reach it before it closes ...

I throw myself on my knees, wrenching at the panel, forcing it up with straining fingers –

It's working. Slowly, slowly, I force it up. There'll be room, just enough room, for me to get out. It'll be all right.

Half crawling, half rolling, I squeeze out under the panel. I feel the edge of it scrape me as I go.

I roll clear. I'm out. Safe.

Once again, joy fills me. My face is wet with tears of relief. I'm free.

I get to my feet and look around.

And then my heart turns over.

Because I haven't, after all, escaped. It was a trap.

I'm standing in a courtyard. On every side of me, on all four sides, are high, grey walls. There are rows and rows of windows, all closed, staring silently down at me.

I can't breathe. This is a place of such terror for me, this courtyard. It holds every bit of terror in the world for me.

Someone's hammering. *Tap – tap – tap.* The sound echoes hollowly round the grey walls.

I look round wildly. There's no one. I'm standing utterly alone in this courtyard.

But again I hear it.

Tap – tap – tap – tap – tap –

And suddenly I know with complete certainty what this courtyard is.

It's an execution yard.

There's going to be an execution here, in this courtyard. Any minute now. They're hammering in the post at this moment. *Tap – tap – tap –*

Then they'll bring the prisoner out. For the first time, I notice an archway in one corner. They'll bring the prisoner out through that archway, hands fastened back, marching between soldiers. They'll tie the prisoner to the post with leather straps. Bind the prisoner's eyes.

And then there'll be an execution.

And I'll have to watch it. That's why I'm here.

I can't escape.

No ... I *will* escape ... I will. Wake up ...

WAKE UP –

Chapter Ten

I'd have given a lot next morning not to be going to work.

After the dream, I'd lain awake for hours, staring into the darkness, forcing my eyes to stay open. I must have dropped into an exhausted doze around dawn because Dad had to shake me awake when he brought me a cup of tea.

'Time to get up, son, if you don't want to be late.' He pulled back the curtains, letting in a flood of light that made me cover my eyes with a groan. 'They've just said on the radio it could be the hottest day for fifty years,' he added.

I thought with dread of the morning ahead in the Coulson Arms' kitchen. The ovens and hobs and fryer were always on at full force.

'Are you all right, Nick?' Dad was looking at me anxiously.

'Yes.' I swung my feet to the floor. 'Look, I've got to hurry. Kirsty will be waiting.'

'Make sure you have something to eat before you go.'

'No time, Dad.' I couldn't have eaten anything. 'Maybe when I get there ...'

I leaned over the parapet of the bridge by the Quay, waiting for the car. The sun was already beating on my back. I envied the swans as they glided through the shadowy arch, their five cygnets grown into shaggy teenagers now. They looked so cool and untroubled.

What had last night's dream meant? And why had it come that particular night?

I'd been so much happier; I'd almost forgotten the dream world of corridors and fear. It was as if I needed to be nudged back into awareness because I'd grown too used to the dreams. I had to be shown a new terror. The courtyard.

I shivered in the hot sunshine. I wouldn't think about the courtyard. I couldn't.

But I couldn't stop my mind going back to it once I was in the back seat of the car and heading through the narrow lanes towards the Coulson Arms. Weeks of sun and drought had scorched the grass verges a dry gingery-brown. The leaves of the trees hung down, waiting for rain.

'Hey, Nick! Wake up. You're not listening.'

'What? Oh, sorry, Beryl. What did you say?'

Beryl, the chambermaid who always travelled with Kirsty, had swung round in her seat to talk to me.

'Show him, Kirsty. The boy's half asleep this morning.'

Kirsty flapped her left hand over her shoulder. An engagement ring sparkled.

'Ah – yes, I see. Congratulations, Kirsty.'

'Thanks, Nick.' She laughed. 'Jeff and I still haven't got used to the idea ourselves. We only decided last night. We were walking along Bournemouth sea front, you see –'

Tap – tap – tap ... The sound hammered in my mind, drowning out the voices from the front of the car. *Tap – tap – tap* ...

I shook my head to chase the sound away. In front, the conversation had switched to the weather.

'... it's all right for you, Beryl,' Kirsty was saying. 'You can lock yourself in an empty bathroom

74

somewhere and take a cold shower. I have to look cool and calm for Mr Briggs's guests today. He's having an important business lunch in the restaurant. Some sort of deal's in the air.'

'Nothing will worry you today,' Beryl said. She turned back to me again.

'Not spending the day there, are you, Nick? Haven't you noticed? We're here.'

Tap – tap – tap. The sound of hammering echoed round the empty courtyard as I followed them across the hotel car park to the kitchen door. Hammering for a death.

It wasn't as difficult as I'd feared. There just wasn't time to think.

First, there was the usual stack of breakfast dishes to do. Then Chef started preparing a special lunch for Mr Briggs's guests and passed me all the dirty pans. Then I had to peel half a sack of potatoes, loading them in batches into the machine and watching them tumbling out at the bottom as clean as new-shorn sheep.

The kitchen was steamy-hot. I felt my T-shirt sticking to my back. In no time at all the lunchtime rush began.

'Three Dorset paté, four soups, two plaice and chips ...'

The heat hadn't affected people's appetites. I dashed between the sink, the table and the fryer. By now I'd learned to be in the right place doing the right thing most of the time.

'One scampi, three smoked mackerel, two apple crumbles with custard ...'

My stomach rumbled; there'd been no time for a break today. We wouldn't have our lunch until things slowed down.

Across the kitchen I saw Chef handing over steaming plates to go to the restaurant for Mr Briggs's business lunch. We went on preparing bar snacks.

'Nick! Take out these food orders, please.'

The lounge bar was crowded. All the doors and windows stood open to catch any breeze there might be.

'Number twenty-eight.' I raised my voice above the hubbub. 'Three-chicken-salads, one-ham-and-egg-pie. Number twenty-EIGHT.'

Eventually I found the people sitting at a table out on the grass in front of the building. As I unloaded my tray I glanced up and saw the village, the sea and the sky all merged into one shimmering haze of heat. Car after car was passing down the lane on the way to the beach.

At last the final order was completed. Wearily I turned to the waiting mountain of dirty dishes.

'Hello, slaves.' Kirsty put her head round the kitchen door. Behind her, Jeff was carrying a tray of sparkling drinks. 'It's celebration time.'

Mrs Baldwin looked questioningly at Chef.

'Oh, you'll have a drink, won't you, Chef?' Kirsty wheedled. 'You must help us celebrate. Everyone's coming ... waiting staff, chambermaids, everybody. You've all earned a drink, working so hard in the heat. Go on, Chef. Mr Briggs'll never know. He's still at lunch in the restaurant.'

She began handing round glasses. 'And you, young Nick.' She tweaked my apron undone. 'Leave those dishes now.'

A glass was pushed into my hand. I took a cautious sip and spluttered.

'Wh – What is it?'

'Don't ask,' Jeff said. 'Just drink it up, right?'

76

The kitchen began filling up with people. Some-one had a radio and Kirsty and Jeff began dancing to the throb of the music. Even Chef was leaning against the wall smiling austerely over the rim of his glass.

'Have another, Nick.' Jeff reached out an arm and poured.

'Okay.' This time I could swallow it without spluttering. 'Thanks.' I took a couple of big gulps and felt it sparkling all the way down.

'Better eat something with it.' A bag of crisps was tossed in my direction.

Someone had given Kirsty and Jeff a present. Kirsty unwrapped it and draped the silver tinsel ribbon round my shoulders. Jeff filled my glass again. The kitchen babbled with laughter and movement and music. I was beginning to feel good.

'Where's Beryl?' Kirsty stopped suddenly in the middle of the floor. 'She promised to come.'

'She must've forgotten the time.' One of the other chambermaids, perched on the table, looked up from her conversation. 'I'll go and find her.'

'No, sit there.' Kirsty looked round. 'Nick'll go. Won't you, Nick?'

'It'll sober him up,' Jeff suggested, grinning.

'Okay.' I drained my glass and held it out for a refill. 'As long as I can take this with me. Where do I go?'

'Up to the first floor,' said the chambermaid. 'Beryl's working in room 107 or 108 ... somewhere around there. You'll find her.'

'Right.' Carrying my glass, I went out to the lounge bar. Even though food orders had finished a few people were still there, drinking and chatting. I made for the stairs.

Kirsty came hurrying after me.

'No, no, Nick. You're not supposed to use the main staircase. Turn round.'

Giggling, I allowed her to steer me across the room.

'Whoops.' My feet didn't seem to want to co-operate. I took another gulp from my glass.

'Really, Nick. Anyone would think you'd been on the hard stuff. Straighten yourself up, will you?' She knotted my tinsel firmly under my chin.

'That's better. Now – go and fetch Beryl.'

She pointed to a shabby brown door in the corner next to the bar. 'Right, see that door? You *can* see, Nick, can't you?'

I rolled my eyes wildly. 'Um ... yes. Think so.'

'Right. That leads to the back stairs. When you get to the top, just follow the room numbers till you get to 107 and 108. Off you go.'

She gave me a push that made me stumble and giggle. 'And tell Beryl to hurry, or all the drink will have gone.'

'Oh ... shame.' I waggled my half-full glass at her. Then I turned and pushed the door open.

It fell closed behind me.

All the noise and laughter and bright lights were left on the other side.

I stood for a minute in the shadowy dark, clutching my wine glass. Then I groped my way to the foot of the stairs and began climbing.

It was completely quiet.

Did I already know, deep down, what I was going to see at the top?

I think I must have done. Because the bubbly, giggling feeling had suddenly gone. To be replaced by cold fear.

'What's the matter?' I found myself whispering

78

aloud as I climbed. 'What's the matter?'

This was simply an old, shabby staircase. Its treads were covered with pock-marked green lino; the wooden handrail and the beige walls were sticky with grubby fingerprints. It was very different from the main hotel stairs, the ones Kirsty had stopped me using, with their thick carpet and shining white banisters. But this fear was more – much more – than that. The wine glass shook in my hand, and my heart was cold with dread.

Dread? Dread of what?

At the top of the stairs was another door. Closed.

I paused. Then, heart hammering, I opened it.

The wine glass slipped from my fingers and I stood still, looking. First one way and then the other.

The corridors. The corridors of my dreams.

I started to walk. To the left? To the right? I don't know; it could have been either.

Doors lined the corridors on either side, painted the same creamy-white as the walls. There was no one around. It was very quiet. My feet made no sound on the thick, soft carpet. The air was thick and soft too. I couldn't breathe properly.

Was it real? Was it a dream? There was no longer any difference. Reality and dreams had fused into one, as I'd always known that one day they would. And now it had happened.

I began to run.

This corridor wasn't straight for long; I had to turn a corner. I ran on, and there was another corner. Once, I stumbled on two or three shallow steps going down. I picked myself up and went on running.

And then I heard it.

Someone was laughing. and calling me. I didn't hear

the words, just the voice, but I knew I was the one being called. Someone was calling and teasing and laughing.

Where? Behind me? ... No, in front. Or was it only in my head?

I had to obey the voice.

No, I mustn't. That was dangerous. I had to get out.

My hand touched a door handle. That's where the voice was coming from, from inside that room. I hesitated.

Then I flung open the door.

And stood in the doorway, gaping.

There was no hanging white cloth. No giant face laughing at me. There was nothing but a perfectly ordinary, unoccupied hotel bedroom.

Two beds stood side by side, covered with smooth blue bedspreads. There was built-in white furniture, a spotless wash basin, mirrors. Everything was clean, tidy, impersonal.

I went on standing there, panting for breath.

And the voice came once more, calling me and laughing.

I crossed the room in three strides and wrenched back the net curtains from the window.

This room looked out at the back of the building, on to the lawns and rock gardens that I'd seen on the day of my interview with Mr Briggs. Today they were bathed in summer heat. Directly below me I saw the sun terrace with its tubs of flowers, its low stone wall and its three steps down to the lawn guarded by the stone lion.

And my heart turned over.

For astride the lion was the girl. She was wearing a purple T-shirt and blue jeans cut off raggedly at the knee, and she was crouching low over his stone mane,

80

her hands and knees and heels urging him on like a racehorse, while her shining black hair bounced up and down on her shoulders with the excitement of her unseen gallop.

Then she turned and looked straight at the window where I was standing, and I saw that she was laughing and laughing and laughing.

Chapter Eleven

There was no time to think about what I'd seen. This time I had to catch her.

I flung myself across the bedroom and raced back along the corridor. As I reached the door at the head of the stairs, my foot sent my forgotten wine glass spinning away and I heard it shatter. I thudded down the stairs and burst through the brown door at the bottom.

'Nick, look out—'

I collided with a barmaid going past with a tray of empty glasses.

'Sorry ...'

Across the lounge and out into the blinding sun.

My hip caught the corner of one of the tables on the grass outside as I tore round the front of the hotel, and I heard someone shout after me. But I was already out of earshot, pounding down the narrow path next to the churchyard, heading for the terrace at the back.

Round one more corner and I pulled up, panting.

The lion's paws were planted foursquare on top of the wall. It gazed ahead with its usual aloof expression. Its back, dipped like a saddle, was empty.

'*Damn.*' I stamped the terrace in angry frustration. 'Why do you keep doing this to me? *Why* can't I catch you, damn you, damn you ...' I kicked out at one of the flower tubs, overturning it.

'I'll catch you if it's the last thing I ever do. How dare you ... how dare you ...'

In my rage, I ran across the lawn and started dragging plants aside, trampling all over them in a frenzy of searching.

'I'll catch you ... Come out. Where are you hiding? ... You're not hiding from me this time –'

There was a sharp rapping sound behind me. Reluctantly, I looked round.

Mr Briggs was standing at a window of the restaurant. He was beckoning me urgently.

I ran across and in through the open restaurant door. A ring of people were seated round a table by the window.

'Have you seen her?' I was gasping for breath and bathed in sweat. 'Is she here? A girl in a purple T-shirt ... blue jeans. Only a minute or two ago.'

Their faces were frozen, uncomprehending. A man with dark shaggy eyebrows frowned and said, 'What? What's that?'

'She was out there. Just now.' I gestured at the terrace. 'On the lion ...'

'*Nicholas.*' Mr Briggs came up behind me. 'What do you think –'

'It's no good.' I began running again. 'She's not here. She must be in the lounge ... somewhere ...'

I ran across the restaurant and out into the passage. I flung open the kitchen door.

'Is she here?' I shouted above the din.

All their faces turned to me, startled.

'Who? Beryl, do you mean?' Kirsty shook her head. 'No, we haven't –' but I'd already slammed the door on them and gone back through to the lounge again.

I half collapsed over the bar, arms outstretched, summoning enough breath to speak.

'A girl,' I managed to get out, 'a girl in a purple –'

83

'Out of the way, Nick,' the barmaid hissed. 'I'm serving this gentleman. Can't you see?'

'Oh – Oh, yes. But it's urgent. I need to find her. She's wearing a purple T-shirt and –'

With one hand, she pushed me aside while she placed a tray of coffee in front of the customer.

'Sorry about that. That'll be one pound fifty, please.'

My face was throbbing with heat. 'I've *got* to find her.'

I pushed myself up and went right round the lounge, checking every group of people, every dim corner. There was no sign of her.

'Outside ... She must be outside.'

I ran out of the front door. Down the village street. I couldn't even call her. What name would I call?

My foot caught a rough paving stone and I nearly went sprawling, but I recovered myself and went on running. Heat was beating up from the road. A black and white dog stretched out in the shade, tongue lolling. Cars jostled in the narrow street, on their way to and from the beach, the people inside them flushed and uncomfortable in the afternoon sun.

'I must find her ...' I was almost sobbing with frustration.

I saw a sign: VILLAGE STORES AND POST OFFICE. It was a last hope. She could be in there, buying sweets or something. Hadn't she been eating sweets the first time I'd ever seen her, that day on the school bus?

I ran across the street ... and straight into Jeff.

'Nick ... There you are.' He held me in a firm grip. 'Have you gone crazy or something?'

I tried to pull myself free. 'There's a girl. I've got to find a girl. She –'

He laughed. 'No girls for you, Nick, my lad. Mr

Briggs sent me to find you. He wants to see you in his office. Pronto. If not before.'

As we crossed the hotel car park Mr Briggs was there, seeing off his guests. He gave me a short stare, then went on chatting and shaking hands, but I felt everyone's eyes on me and quailed inside.

The reception hall was cool and quiet. Rather hopelessly, I tried to straighten my hair and my clothes. Then Mr Briggs came striding in.

'Thank you, Jeff,' was all he said. 'Get back to work now.' For me, there was only a curt nod before he vanished into the office.

Jeff gave me a quizzical look. 'I'd get rid of this, Nick, before you go in. Might help.' He reached out and removed Kirsty's piece of tinsel from around my neck and held it out to me. 'Want it?'

Numbly, I shook my head. He dropped it on the table. 'Well … good luck anyway.'

'Thanks,' I said. Then I walked over to the office and tapped on the door.

Three minutes later, I'd been dismissed from the Coulson Arms.

Chapter Twelve

'We must be getting a bit nearer,' said Granny. 'Can you see what the hold-up is, Nick?'

I wound down my window and put my head out. A drizzle of fine rain blew into my face. I blinked to clear my vision and saw wet car roofs snaking into the distance between the high Devon hedges. Clouds of exhaust hung in the damp air.

'Not yet,' I reported, winding up the window again. 'It must be road works or an accident. There's a long way to go yet, whatever it is.'

'We'll just have to wait, then,' Granny said philosophically, edging the car a few metres forward and switching off the engine. She looked in the mirror at the back seat. 'Hungry, Dan?'

Daniel said, 'Mm,' without lifting his head from his current Roald Dahl. He'd brought a stack of them with him for this holiday at Granny's in Plymouth, and happily buried himself in them at odd times, chortling quietly as he read.

I'd spent quite a lot of the holiday reading, too. I'd discovered a collection of my mother's old childhood books in Granny's spare room. Some of them had her signature on the fly leaf: *Joyce Mary Pendeen*, Mum's name before she married Dad. In the week that I'd been there I'd got through three *Biggles* books, two *William* books, half a dozen *Rupert* annuals and a *Bumper Book of Girls' School Stories*.

They helped. I couldn't seem to manage anything

more demanding. I read mainly at night, making my eyes stay open, determined not to slip into sleep and find myself back in that courtyard. The nights were very long.

'... and to think it's still August,' Granny was saying, flicking on the windscreen wipers to clear the view. 'But we had a good drive over Dartmoor. The heather's at its best just now. And you liked the ponies, didn't you, Dan?'

'Yes, great.'

'That was quite a nice place we stopped for lunch, wasn't it, Nick? I suppose the hotel where you were working – the Coulson Arms, was it? – was rather similar?'

'No heather,' I said. 'No ponies. But yes. Sort of similar.'

She switched on and moved a little further. 'It was a shame you had to leave. I was sorry to hear about it from Joyce.'

It was the first time either of us had mentioned the Coulson Arms. She hadn't once asked me why I'd changed my mind so suddenly about wanting to come and stay with her; she'd simply welcomed me as warmly as ever. I'd always loved staying there. When I'd been little, she and Grandad had taken me off to all the beaches in Devon and Cornwall for long days of sandcastles and ice cream and paddling. Even now, with Grandad gone, Plymouth was still everything that was safe and happy and comforting.

'Yes,' I said. 'It was rather a shame.'

She looked at me. 'Do you want to tell me about it?'

'Well –' I shifted uncomfortably in my seat. 'There was a party, you see. In the kitchen. The boss man didn't like it. He said –'

'He asked you to leave, is that – Ah, just a minute,

Nick.' She switched on the engine. 'We're moving.'

For the next few minutes she was busy taking us past road works, with their lines of traffic cones and sodden men working. Then, when we were speeding along once more towards Plymouth, she remarked,

'Drink's difficult stuff to handle, of course, when you're young.'

'Yes,' I said. I didn't say any more.

But, although I didn't want to, I couldn't help remembering ...

Mr Briggs's face was disdainful as he faced me across his desk and listed my crimes. I'd interrupted his lunch party; I'd damaged his garden; I'd left a trail of destruction all round the hotel, including enough broken glass to cut Beryl's foot when she'd been going downstairs soon after me. I'd run all the way down the village street ... And all this at a time when I should have been working.

'I'm sorry, Mr Briggs. I—'

He raised his hand. 'Sorry isn't enough. It's clear to me that you've been drinking. Your whole appearance ... your behaviour tells me that. It was totally irresponsible and I blame other people too for giving it to you. You know quite well that any under-age drinking is against my rules.' His eyes bored into me and I squirmed. 'But especially when you are supposed to be on duty.'

He sighed. 'I shall send you money in lieu of notice, of course, and any necessary documentation. Meanwhile, I should like you to leave at once.'

I felt numb ... confused. 'You mean – this afternoon?'

'I mean right away. Don't you understand? You're being dismissed.'

88

'But –' My brain wouldn't catch up. 'I always help Mrs Baldwin wash the kitchen floor before I go. And I'll have to wait for Kirsty. She gives me a lift home.'

'No.' He reached out to the phone. He said into it, 'Taxi. Coulson Arms. As soon as you can, please.'

He looked at me. 'The kitchen is being cleared up at this minute. I hope everyone understands that celebrations of any kind need my approval in future. Off you go. You may wait in Reception until the taxi arrives to take you home. Your fare will be paid, of course.'

'Thank you.' There didn't seem anything else to say.

I stood in the hall, waiting, twisting the discarded piece of tinsel in my fingers, and feeling nothing much at all.

In about ten minutes, the taxi came.

I was just climbing into it when there was a rush of footsteps on the gravel.

'Oh, Nick.' Kirsty threw herself on me. 'I'm so sorry. It's all my fault.' She was nearly in tears. 'I tried to tell him.'

'Tell him what?'

'About your drinks, of course.'

'My drinks?' I said. 'What about my drinks?'

'Well, that they weren't alcoholic, of course. They were different from everyone else's. They were that sparkling stuff that looks like wine but isn't.'

She saw my face. 'Oh, come on, Nick. We wouldn't buy you alcohol and get you into trouble. Surely you knew you weren't drinking alcohol? I thought you were just pretending.'

'Of course I was.' I remembered how I'd giggled and staggered about. Somehow, the stuff had gone to my head. It must have been the power of suggestion or something. 'I was just kidding.'

'We're all terribly upset. Mrs Baldwin ... Beryl ... Chef.'

'*Chef*?'

'Yes, of course. Everyone. Jeff says we ought to go on strike till Briggs takes you back.'

I shook my head. 'He'd never do that. You'd just lose your jobs as well, probably.'

She gave me a quick hug. 'We'll miss you,' she said. 'Keep in touch, Nick.'

The taxi carried me off. I turned once and saw the thatched cottages straggling down to the sea. Then we reached the top of the long hill, and the village and the Coulson Arms were left behind.

As it was our last evening in Plymouth, Granny took Daniel and me to a Chinese restaurant. Afterwards, we strolled on the Hoe, the huge grassy area above the sea. It was just getting dark.

Daniel ran ahead to the lighthouse. Granny tucked her arm through mine and we walked in silence for a few minutes.

'There'll be other jobs,' she said at last. 'Other chances.'

'Mm,' I said. 'I suppose so.'

She looked at me sideways. 'What did Joyce and Roger have to say about it?'

'Oh,' I said. 'Not much really.'

I thought back.

The taxi had taken me through the narrow lanes towards home. I stared blindly out of the windows, trying to think how on earth to break the news to Mum and Dad.

And then, when it happened, it had been a anti-climax.

They were in the shop, of course. It was full of

customers. Mum gave me a startled look as I walked through and glanced at her watch, but she and Dad had to carry on serving. I went through to the kitchen and made some tea.

A postcard had come for me, a picture of two rather depressed-looking Highland cattle in the rain. I turned it over. *Didn't get to Florida after all*, was scrawled on the back, *so haven't met M. Mouse, D. Duck or S. White after all. Next summer maybe. Will bring you a haggis next term*.

Oh, well. At least Phil seemed to be talking to me again.

I took the tea to the room behind the shop and waited for a lull. At last they came out and I poured them a mug each. I gave them time for a sip or two. Then I said,

'Guess what I lost today?'

Mum looked at me. 'What?' she asked.

I drew a deep breath. 'My job,' I said. 'Lost it just like that.' I snapped my fingers. Oh, help, I thought. Why am I being so flippant?

Dad's head jerked up. 'You've what? Whatever happened, Nick?'

'Well, I –' I hesitated – Mum's face was buried in her mug. 'I –' Then I chickened out.

'I was sort of made redundant,' I said. 'You know, they're cutting down the workforce. That's what Briggs said. He's making the place more competitive. So he picked on me.' I shrugged. 'You know what they say, Dad. Last in, first out. And I was last in.'

'But –' Dad looked at Mum. 'This Briggs chap can't do that, can he? What's his phone number? I'll get on to him right away. He'd promised the boy a job for the whole holiday.'

'Roger.' Mum pulled his arm. 'Wait. We need to talk about it ...'

'But—'

'Dad, don't,' I said. 'Don't phone him.' I could already hear the conversation between him and Briggs in my head, could hear Briggs telling him about the chase round the hotel, the damage I'd done. I cringed.

'It was only a temporary job, Dad, after all. I've got to go back to school in a week or two anyway. Don't bother.'

And, eventually, that was that. Nothing more was said.

'Granny, don't worry about Mum and Dad.' I squeezed her arm. 'They didn't seem to mind much.'

I felt her relax. 'Well, if you're sure ... I expect that's the best way. Put it all behind you. As I said, darling, there'll be plenty of other jobs.'

But on the coach going home to Dorset the next morning, my thoughts turned again to the Coulson Arms.

It wasn't just that I'd lost my job in disgrace; it was much more than that. In Plymouth, I'd managed most of the time to shut out the memories of that last day, but now they came flooding back.

I'd found the corridors.

They existed. They weren't just dreams. I'd walked along them. They were at the Coulson Arms.

And the courtyard?

Could that be at the Coulson Arms too?

I glanced at Daniel in the seat beside me. As usual, he was reading. I took a piece of paper from my pocket, and found a pencil. Then, shielding it from Daniel, I drew a quick plan of the Coulson Arms as far as I understood it.

When I'd first gone there for my interview, I'd noticed what a long way back the building went, how much bigger it was than it had looked from the front. It was a big grey block of a building, with many more rooms it in than I'd seen when I went looking for Beryl. Hotel rooms are generally quite small. They couldn't possibly run the full width of the building. That solid-looking square was really a hollow square.

The rooms went all the way round. And at the centre could be – must be – a courtyard of some kind. A courtyard on which their windows looked out.

In my dream, I'd stood alone at the edge of the courtyard and the hammering had echoed round the grey walls. Was I dreaming about the Coulson Arms? About a courtyard I'd never seen?

I shivered. They'd been preparing an execution.

Whose execution? Who was that prisoner who was to be led out from under the archway to the post and blindfolded?

The courtyard was drawing me into itself, calling me as the voice called me in my dreams. I had to obey. I had no choice, despite my terror of the place.

I had to go in search of it. There was no other way to be free of the dreams, or of that girl on the lion's back, laughing into the empty air.

I knew that, deep inside myself, without understanding it in the least.

Chapter Thirteen

My opportunity came two days later.

'Hello, Nick.' It was Alison, Cathy's friend from school, just about to go into the library. 'What are you doing down here?'

'Just mooching round,' I said. Since getting back from Plymouth I'd spent most of the time sitting about in my room, thinking about the courtyard and how I had to go and find it. 'Actually, I'll be quite glad to go back to school next week. How about you?'

'Oh, I'm really busy,' she said. 'As a matter of fact, now I've caught you, perhaps you'd like to sign this.' She produced a long list of signatures.

'What is it?'

'You could be one of my sponsors. We're doing a project at youth club to raise money for Save the Children.'

'What sort of project? I don't sponsor just anything, you know.'

'It's called S.A.N.D.'

'Meaning?'

'Sponsored All Night Disco,' she explained. 'It's tonight, from eight to eight. There's still time to pledge some money. We do the rest. We keep dancing for twelve hours non-stop – well, virtually non-stop – and if I'm still on my feet at eight tomorrow morning, you pay up. It's all properly organised. I've got masses of sponsors – look. I'm just going in the library because my mum works there and she's getting all the staff to sign. Oh, go on, Nick. Just twenty pence or something.'

I took the pencil she was holding out to me. Then I handed it back.

'No,' I said. 'But you've sold me the idea. See you tonight at eight.'

It was a rush, but I managed it. By ten to eight that evening, I was walking into the youth club. I showed my new membership card at the door.

'Nick! I didn't know you were a member.' Alison came over with a group of friends.

'Oh, yes,' I said.

'Since when?'

'Since four o'clock this afternoon. I decided to join. And I've gone straight into action. Get a look at this.'

My list of sponsors wasn't quite as long as Alison's but it was plenty long enough. The good thing about living all my life in one town was I knew a lot of people. It was amazing how many I'd managed to persuade in two or three hours.

'My dad wasn't too keen to sign at the beginning,' I said. 'He thought we ought to be doing something more useful with our time, like decorating old people's kitchens or digging their gardens.'

'Difficult at night,' someone said.

'We're going to do something like that next,' said Alison. 'And this is for Save the Children.'

'Yes, I know,' I said. 'He signed in the end.'

The youth club leader stood on the stage in a huddle with several teachers from school and the curate from the church. Buffet food was being set out on long trestle tables. A giant clock on the stage, emblazoned with S.A.N.D. banners, showed three minutes to eight.

'Right, everyone,' called the leader. 'In a moment,

we'll be closing the doors. Luckily, we're some way from houses here, but we've had to promise to keep the noise level right down.' There was some mock booing.

'Okay, you all know the rules. No more than three minutes' time out per hour, for refreshments or whatever, or you'll have to be disqualified. Keep going till tomorrow morning at eight, and you'll have earned the money you've got pledged. Then we'll all sit down to breakfast, and then go home to bed. So take it easy for the first hour or two. Don't overdo it. We're in for a long, long night.'

You can say that again, I thought, my heart sinking as the music began. I'd never been one of nature's natural disco-ers. That was more in Daniel's line than mine. But it was going to be worth it.

Have you ever been up all night? I mean, *all night*?

I'd thought I was the world expert on sleeplessness, but I learned something the night of the S.A.N.D. However long the hours seem when you're lying in bed, it's nothing – absolutely nothing – compared with how long they seem spent in a large room with fifty-odd other people, all of them trying to stay on their feet and do something that'll pass as 'dancing'. I realised for the first time that even on my worst dream nights, I must actually have done quite a lot of dozing. Dozing wasn't allowed at S.A.N.D.

'Come on, everyone!' About once an hour, the leader's cheery voice cut into our trance-like state. 'It's conga time!'

Or – 'Hokey-Cokey, everybody!' Even, once or twice, Oranges and Lemons. Anything to keep us moving.

Grumbling, protesting, we allowed ourselves to be pushed through the formations. Then it was back to our droopy, elderly shuffle that, in contrast, seemed almost as restful as falling into bed. Time ceased to have any meaning; unimaginable that it would ever end.

There were breaks, of course. A gulp of coffee or Coke, a hurried visit to the loos, an occasional moment of cold night air at the door. Then more shuffling ... slow turning ... shuffling ... as the music throbbed and wailed.

Perhaps I would have gone on for ever, mole-like, if Alison hadn't lifted her head from a huddle of shoulders all supporting each other and said,

'Look, everybody. Morning.'

It wasn't, of course. Just a square of grey at the windows instead of the black that had been there for so long. But it was enough.

'We're going to make it! Only another two or three hours. We'll make it.'

I lifted my head. 'No,' I said. 'Sorry. Not me.' I walked quietly, a little stiffly, towards the door.

'Nick, don't give up now.'

'Sorry,' I said again.

At the door, they tried to rally me with offers of food, a drink, a minute or two's rest. I shook my head. That was it. Finished. Sorry.

Then I was outside in the cool, grey end of night, picking up my bicycle, wheeling it to the road. I rubbed my hand once over my face, glanced at the sky, heard a lorry grinding up a hill somewhere far away.

Then I mounted my bike and set off to ride to the Coulson Arms.

Devious; complicated. Certainly exhausting.

But it worked. That was all that mattered.

At home, Mum and Dad always got up early, very

early, to be ready for the first of the day's deliveries of bread and cakes. From then on, they were constantly bustling between the shop and the back room, passing the foot of the stairs all the time as they checked invoices, counted out orders, arranged window displays. It would have been completely impossible for me to creep past them unseen. Any wild ideas I'd had about knotted sheet ropes out of bedroom windows had to be left where they belonged – in the pages of fiction. Anyway, even if I'd got out, Dad would have found my bed empty when he took my usual cup of tea up at seven. There was no chance I was going to be back by then.

But S.A.N.D. had provided the perfect cover.

For I had to go to the Coulson Arms very early in the day. I knew that. I'd been dismissed in disgrace; I had no right to be there any more. The risk of bumping into Briggs during the daytime, or late into the night, was only too high. But the morning ... very, very early in the morning ... when the hotel was the quietest, with the guests still asleep and most of the staff had not yet arrived for work. That's when I could hope to move through the hotel undetected.

I pedalled on through the dim lanes, meeting no one. The air was damp and chill with dew.

Slowly, it grew less dark. As I dismounted at the foot of the last hill and began to push my bike up, I noticed the hedgerows had taken on a faint tinge of colour. Turning, I saw a smudge of orange in the eastern sky.

Chapter Fourteen

I came to the top of the hill and saw the village below me, its thatched cottages sleeping in the dawn. Beyond, the sea was shrouded in white mist.

I noticed an open farm gate, leaning half off its hinges, the grass on either side of it thick and undisturbed. I dragged my bike inside and concealed it as well as I could in the hedge. Then I went on on foot, my trainers making no sound on the road. I drew level with the Coulson Arms a minute or two before six.

I skirted the gravel car park, holding my breath. I had no detailed plan in mind, only a deep conviction that all this was what I must do. And here I had a small piece of luck.

They must have been having some structural work done of some kind, because a large builder's skip stood close to the kitchen door. Silently, I went to stand behind it, so that I was shielded from the view of anyone coming towards the door.

And then I waited.

A bird uttered three sharp notes. Another joined it. The light was strong now; the day was coming all too quickly. *Now*, I thought fiercely, my body silent, unmoving. *Now*.

Six-fifteen. Nothing happened. Late, this morning of all mornings.

Two, three minutes passed.

Then I heard it. Footsteps hurrying towards me across the gravel. I drew in even further to the wall.

I saw her white plastic carrier bag and the edge of her green coat. Heard her rapid breathing. She was fumbling with her key.

'Drat it.' She stooped to pick it up. Inserted it in the lock. Went inside.

And left the door open.

I let out my breath. Then I slipped inside the dimly lit lobby and crouched behind some old folding tables that were always stored there.

Mrs Baldwin came back without her coat and bag, buttoning her overall. I heard her close the outside door and drop the latch. Then her footsteps went back to the kitchen.

My hands were sweating. This was going to be the riskiest moment.

But I'd guessed correctly. As I silently crossed the corner of the kitchen and went out to the lounge, I caught a glimpse of her back through the open door of the cold store. She was fetching the trays of bacon that had been laid out overnight ready for her to put into the oven for early breakfasts. I threw up a prayer of thanks for the hours of kitchen chat I'd listened to during my weeks at the Coulson Arms, which had left me knowing Mrs Baldwin's working routine nearly as well as I'd known my own.

I went across the lounge on tiptoe. The bar itself was enclosed by a locked security grid to deter burglars. But my attention was on the brown door next to it.

I turned the handle and it opened. Of course, it was probably an emergency fire exit for the guests upstairs.

I began to climb the stairs quietly. And now I had to fight the fear that waited there for me, the same fear that had engulfed me the first time. Swallowing hard, I went on climbing.

I pushed open the door at the top and closed it softly behind me. For just one moment, I hesitated. Then I began walking.

The carpet muffled my footfalls but, even so, a floorboard creaked once or twice and sent a dart of panic up my spine. But there was no sound from behind the closed doors on either side. It was as if the dead slept behind them.

Was anyone even there, asleep? Or was every room empty, like the one I'd burst into last time, making all this elaborate caution ridiculous? But even as I thought that, a sharp hard cough – a man's cough – came from behind one of the doors.

Forcing myself not to run, I rounded a corner. There was another stretch of corridor exactly the same. I walked along it steadily, heart pounding. Someone inside one of the rooms was snoring.

Another corner; another stretch of corridor, one that passed the head of the main staircase. Another corner; another stretch.

One final corner and I was back where I'd begun, at the top of the back stairs. Now I understood the layout on that floor. It was, as I'd expected, a square.

And the square was hollow. It had to be. The room I'd run into last time was one of the ones on my left; that had overlooked the back garden. All the left-hand rooms looked outward like that, facing the garden or the church or the sea and so on. But the rooms on my right couldn't do that. What did their windows look out on?

I moistened my lips.

There was only one answer.

They faced inwards. They looked at each other across a courtyard.

As soon as I'd thought this, I began to shake. It was one thing to work it out in theory, quite another to be faced with it and know it for certain. I couldn't pretend any longer that everything might be coincidence, mere chance. The dreams and the reality matched too well.

I'd dreamed about a girl ... and then I'd seen her. I'd dreamed about some corridors, and then I'd found them. I'd dreamed about a courtyard—

And now it was here. On the other side of these rooms.

An execution yard.

I started to walk round the square once more. This time I looked only at the right-hand side. I noticed bathrooms placed at intervals. And when I had nearly completed the square I saw, next to a bathroom, a door marked *Private*.

I looked inside. It was a little utility room with a sink, cupboards, brooms and mops. The chambermaids probably used it to store their stuff. In one corner at the back was a door.

There'd been so many doors. But this would be the last.

I pushed it; pulled at it. It didn't move. I shook the handle, tugged, put my shoulder to it.

Then I saw a key, on a shelf at eye level.

Trembling, I fitted it. It turned with a click that split the silence. I waited for someone to come and apprehend me.

When no one came, I pushed the door and it gave. A flight of dusty concrete steps led out under a grey stone archway. A chill hung over everything.

One. Two. Three steps down. Like a prisoner. *Four. Five. Six. Seven. Eight. Nine.*

Ten.

I stood in the archway and slowly, slowly, made

myself look, though this place held for me all the terror in the world.

The high grey walls of the building enclose it all the way round. The ground is paved with grey stone slabs. The whole courtyard is empty. Silent. I'm utterly alone.

Rows of windows stare down at me, their curtains drawn. Window after window after window.

There is only one which has no curtains. Only one in all the rows.

The girl is standing there, looking down at me through the glass. For the first time — the only time — she isn't laughing, she isn't smiling, she's white-faced, looking down at me standing in the courtyard. And there is such sadness, such grief in her face, that my whole body is turned to ice.

'No.' I back towards the steps, my knuckles pressed against my mouth. '*No.*'

I stumble up the steps, fumble to relock the door at the top and grope my way to the main staircase. I reach for its white newel post like a swimmer drowning.

At the bottom, on the far side of the reception hall, the front doors are propped open. Sunshine is streaming across the red carpet. Someone, just out of sight, is using a vacuum cleaner.

I am out into the morning. Running.

But not in pursuit of the girl. Never again, never, never again ... trying to catch her, trying to speak to her. I've been so slow. I hadn't understood ... understood anything ... anything at all.

Chapter Fifteen

The pebbles clashed and rattled under my feet as I trudged across the empty beach. The sea was very calm, the waves turning over quietly, drawing back. Turning; drawing back. The tide was on its way out, I thought. By the time the day's holidaymakers started arriving there would be plenty of sand uncovered for them.

I glanced up. I could still see the long white road – the road I'd just run all the way down – snaking up to the village between green fields. At the top of the village stood the Coulson Arms. I turned away and went on ploughing my way across the beach.

In a few minutes I couldn't go any further because I'd reached the edge of the cove and the cliffs reared up ahead of me. A couple of fishing boats were upturned on a ramp, and seagulls circled the scattered ropes and lobster pots.

Half a dozen seaweed-stained concrete steps led up from the beach to a toilet block and a refreshment kiosk. ICES, it said. BEACH GOODS. TEAS. I went and sat on the top step and looked over my shoulder. Good, the village was hidden from me now.

A fishing boat was crossing the bay. The throb of its engine just reached me. I squinted into the sun and watched the thin wake behind it grow longer and longer, until the boat rounded the headland and slipped out of sight.

The bumping sound of a vehicle behind me made me

jerk round. A red pick-up truck had parked next to the toilets and a man was unloading buckets and mops.

He nodded at me.

'Mornin'.'

'Hello.'

He took his stuff into the Gents and I heard him whistling as he started sluicing the floor. The smell of disinfectant mingled in the morning air with those of fish and seaweed.

Presently he transferred to the Ladies. I wondered what would happen if any ladies appeared, but there was no one but me around. Glancing at my watch, I saw with surprise that it was still only half-past seven.

I went on staring at the sea.

'That's got that done.'

The man threw his stuff into the back of the truck. 'Need to do it early this time o' year. Whole place'll be full up with people before you can look round. Still, soon be September, won't it?'

'Mm.' My sense of time seemed to have gone. I'd been up all night, hadn't I? Perhaps that was why I felt so odd. As if I'd been hit rather a lot of times and then put back on my feet.

'You're too early,' the man observed.

'Early?'

He nodded at the kiosk. 'Don't open till nine.'

I couldn't have eaten anything. 'No ... I'm just sitting.'

'Ah.' I could feel him wondering about me. 'Come far?'

'From up there.' I pointed. 'From the hotel.'

'Stayin' there, are you?'

'No.' I hesitated. 'I worked there. But they sacked me.' Why am I telling him all this? I thought.

'Did they, now?' He leaned against the truck and

folded his arms. 'Briggsy, would that be?'

I looked up. 'That's right. Do you know him?'

He gave a short laugh. 'I see him stompin' round the village sometimes. They tell me he's a hard man to work for. Not a bad thing, maybe. Bit different in my day, o' course.'

'Did you work there, then?'

'Oh, yes. Gardener, general handyman.' He laughed again. 'General dogsbody.'

'I worked in the kitchen,' I said.

'Well,' he said, 'you're not the first to have lost your job. Won't be the last neither. I seen them come and go in me time. 'Course, the place has changed hands any number o' times since I was there, when the Rydals ran it. Proper shambles then.'

'Was it?'

'All over the show. Didn't know if they was comin' or goin' half the time. 'Course, Brian Rydal liked a bit too much — you know — ' he mimed someone tipping back a glass. 'Him an' his missis was both the same like that. They was proppin' up the bar most o' the time, instead o' lookin' after things.'

I shifted on the hard step. I was obviously in for a long session of memories.

'Everythin' went to pot once the Rydals came. It hadn't been too bad with the previous bloke. But the Rydals never knew what none of us was supposed to be doin', never took no interest. They wouldn't spend nothin' on the garden. I couldn't keep it up the way it ought to have been. An' that kiddy o' theirs —'

'Kiddy?'

'She just ran wild, all over the place. Half ruined the garden. 'Course, they never looked after her proper, poor little —' He stopped for a moment. 'Well, you know. 'Tweren't right.'

106

After a moment, he went on.

'Treat a kiddy like that, what else can you expect? Completely out o' hand.' He sniffed. 'Used to make my life a misery, I know that.'

'How?' I asked.

'Well, I'll give you just one example. I had to go up in the roof one day, to see to the water tank. The guests been complainin' for days about the noise it were makin', an' finally Brian Rydal got round to tellin' me. An' that little maid o' his, she come by while I'm up there, an' she takes me steps away so I'm stranded. I were up there for three hours. Ran off laughin' like a little devil. Can hear her now.' He paused. 'That were the last straw so far as I were concerned. I left soon after that.' He lapsed into silence.

'She were always up in them corridors, chasin' round. In an' out o' the rooms. No business up there, o' course, but what could I do? She were only a kiddy but she'd give me a mouthful o' cheek if I said anythin'. An' the garden! Even worse out there, tramplin' down all me plants, kickin' up the grass. I tell you, she were just wild. I can see her now, ridin' that lion –'

The world went still. The waves stopped turning.

'Black hair streamin' in the wind. It give me a proper turn the first time I seen her on that lion, kickin' an' urgin' it on. If you ask me, she weren't quite right in the head –'

He broke off.

'Ah, well. Best left now.' He opened the door of the truck. 'I'm off home for a bit o' breakfast. You be all right, will you?'

I got to my feet. The name painted on the side of the truck was *Jack Tillings: General Handyman*.

'Mr –' I cleared my throat. 'Mr Tillings?'

'Yes?'

'How long ago was it that you worked at the Coulson Arms?'

'Oh –' He paused to think. ''Tis a good long time. 'Cos I started up on me own soon after that, an' that must be – well – eleven years ago now.'

He climbed into the driver's seat, slammed the door and looked at me through the open window.

I swallowed. 'Just one more thing,' I said. 'The Rydals' daughter. What was her first name?'

'Why, Sophie,' he said. 'It were Sophie Rydal, weren't it?'

He switched on the engine. 'I'd get home for some breakfast now, if I was you.'

I stood there until the sound of the truck had died on the air. Then I sank back on the step.

Sophie Rydal.

Not Helen Mallory. Of course not. Sophie Rydal.

Eleven years ago.

Later, visitors began to arrive for the day, one car after another coming down the road from the village. I'd seen Jack Tillings's truck come back, and now he was busy supervising the motorists as they parked in the big sloping field at the bottom of the hill.

I went on sitting on a rock at the edge of the sea for a long time, idly dropping pebbles into the water one by one. *Eleven years ago,* I thought.

When at last I turned round, I was startled to find groups of people settled for the day all round me, with more walking down from the car-park field carrying beach bags and folding chairs. The field itself was already half covered by neat lines of cars. I knew I should go home but I didn't want to yet.

I got up stiffly and plodded back along the beach to

the road. Cars were queuing at the entrance to the field.

'Up to the man at the top,' the woman at the gate was saying, taking a motorist's money. 'He'll show you where to park.'

I walked up the field. Jack Tillings was edging a car into line.

'Bit more ...' His hands beckoned. 'Come on ... Bit more. Plenty o' room.'

'Mr Tillings—'

He looked round. 'You still here?'

'Yes.' I followed him as he signalled to the next car.

'In there ... tight as you can ... Bit more.'

'About Sophie Rydal,' I said. 'You were telling me about Sophie Rydal.'

'Hang on.' He went to sort out a woman who was unpacking a basket on the spot where he wanted the next car to go. I followed.

'Come on ... plenty o' room.'

'Mr Tillings—'

He turned. 'Look, why d'you keep on about Sophie Rydal? I told you I left the place, didn't I? You'd have to ask somebody what stayed on after me.'

'Who?' No one I'd worked with had ever mentioned the Rydals.

He paused. Just for a moment, no more cars were coming up the field.

'Well,' he said at last, 'there was that woman what used to be the cook. Mrs Watson. You could talk to her, I s'pose, if you're that interested.'

Mrs Watson. I made a mental note of the name.

'Where can I find her? Does she live in the village?'

'No. Never did.' He beckoned the next car. 'She used to have a room at the hotel, her an' that kid o' hers, what were his name? Timmy ... Jimmy ...

somethin' like that. Come on –' he shouted to the motorist – 'Further'n that. Johnny Watson, that were it.'

'Funny little kid,' he went on when the driver had parked to his satisfaction. 'He used to tag along behind young Sophie all day long. Drove me crazy between the two o' them, screamin' an' yellin' all over the place. Out in the garden –'

I tried to bring him back to the point. 'Mr Tillings, do you know where Mrs Watson is now?'

'No idea,' he said flatly. 'Not in the village, that's for certain.' Then, seeing me crestfallen, he added,

'That's me missis down there takin' the money. You could ask her. Sort o' thing she might know.'

'Thanks. Thanks very much.'

I left him to his cars and went down to talk to Mrs Tillings.

'I'm looking for Mrs Watson,' I said. 'She used to work at the Coulson Arms. She had a little boy called Johnny. Your husband thought you might know where I could find her.'

'Mrs Watson?' The woman tipped some money into the pouch she wore round her waist, waved the car through and contemplated the question. To my relief, she showed no curiosity about why I wanted to know. 'Yes, I remember young Johnny and his mother. She was the cook there, wasn't she?'

'That's right. Do you know where she lives now?'

'Funny you should ask that,' she said. 'Because I bumped into her not so long ago, as it happens. I usually go into town once a week to go round the supermarket, an' I was comin' back across the Quay an' I met her. Hadn't seen her for years. She been livin' in town a long time now. She got married again, she told me ... had another kiddy ...'

I tried not to sound impatient. 'If you could give me her address—'

'Address?' She looked vague. Another car was turning in, the driver's hand holding out money to her.

'I'll tell you where you can find her,' she said over her shoulder. 'There's a shop—now, what's it called?'

The car drove away up the field.

'Forester's,' she said triumphantly. 'That's it. A baker's shop called Forester's, down the bottom o' South Street near the Quay. She told me she's married to the chap what runs that.'

She smiled at me kindly.

'All right, m' dear? You go in there an' ask for Joyce Forester, what used to be Joyce Watson. That's her.'

Chapter Sixteen

Whenever I remember that day, I see it from a great distance, as if I'm in a cinema watching a film.

There's a long white road leading away from the sea, threading its way between green fields. A single figure is plodding up the road. He takes no notice of the cars passing him; he is looking straight ahead. Even when he reaches the village – the sort of village you see on jigsaw puzzles, with a street of thatched cottages and pretty gardens, a square-towered church and a picturesque hotel – he looks at nothing. His feet move mechanically. He passes through the village as if it does not exist and goes on climbing the long hill.

At the top, he goes into a field and recovers a bicycle, and continues his journey towards the town. His feet turn the pedals; his eyes are fixed on the road in front of him.

It is impossible to tell what he is thinking.

Mum, I thought. Mum.

The shock had been too big. I couldn't think anything except that. There was no space in my mind any more for the Coulson Arms, or the corridors, or the courtyard or even Sophie Rydal. Only Mum.

Mum would explain. Mum would put it right. She'd put it all right.

All I had to do was keep pedalling, and stay well into the side because these lanes were narrow and anything could be coming and I mustn't be involved in an accident because I had to get to Mum and when I did everything would be all right because Mum would explain ...

Mum was Joyce Forester, who'd been Joyce Pendeen from Plymouth before she married Dad. She couldn't possibly have been Joyce Watson, with a little boy called Johnny Watson. Not possibly.

I had to get to Mum.

It was nearly eleven o'clock when I finally crossed the river bridge into the town. The pavements were thronged with shoppers. I'd have to go into the shop and get Mum out from behind the counter. However busy they were, I'd have to do that ...

'Nick! Stop, stop. Nick!'

I looked round. The bike wavered. I came to a stop. Waited.

'Nick, are you all right? Thank goodness, Dad and I have been so worried. Where on earth have you been –'

Mum's hair was all over her face. She pushed it back with one hand.

'I've been round and round the town looking for you. Dad went down to the youth club at eight this morning to see how you'd got on, and they said you weren't there. They said you'd dropped out soon after five and they thought you'd gone straight home. Everyone's been – I've been out looking ... not knowing ... I–'

She faltered to a stop, staring at my face.

'Nick? Darling, what is it? Has something happened? It doesn't matter about the disco, really. It's not important.'

She put out her hand but I stepped back.

'Nick?' she said again. 'What is it? What's happened?'

I looked at her. Then, in an odd, harsh voice I hardly recognised as mine, I said, 'Who's Johnny Watson?'

There was a long silence. I hadn't known I was going to say that.

'*What?*' she whispered. 'What did you say?'

'Who's Johnny Watson?' I repeated. 'Where is he? What have you done with him? I want to know, Mum. Tell me. Now.'

She went on standing there, half on the pavement, half in the gutter, while people swirled around us. Then she said,

'Don't you know?'

Stiffly, I shook my head. I said again, 'Tell me.'

'All right, Nick. If that's what you want.'

She gave a sudden sigh and looked me straight in the eyes.

'I haven't done anything with him,' she said. 'He's here in front of me. You're Johnny Watson.'

Chapter Seventeen

Someone had carved SARAH 4 MATTHEW into the wood of the seat. I ran my fingers over the letters. The carver hadn't managed the 'S' very well; it was a back-to-front 'Z'.

I said, 'Mum –'

'Have some more coffee, Nick? There's still some in the flask.'

I shook my head.

'And there's a sausage roll here.' Mum reached into the grot box. 'It's today's, I promise you. It just got squashed a bit.'

'No,' I said. 'Thanks. I've had plenty.'

'Oh, Nick, it wasn't much of a meal. I simply did the flask and grabbed the grot box. But you must eat. You've been up all night and you've ... had a shock. Look, shall we go down and have a proper meal in the town? We don't have to stay up here.'

I looked along the grassy walls, and down at the traffic streaming along the bypass far below us, and at a train just pulling into the station. 'I like it up here,' I said.

An hour earlier we'd stood in the street, Mum and I, staring at one another. *You're Johnny Watson*. It had been said. It hung in the air between us like a stone necklace. Nothing could make it unsaid.

I think we might have gone on standing on that pavement for ever if Mum hadn't suddenly whirled into action.

'Come on,' she said. 'Home. Both of us. Put your bike away, wash your face and meet me outside in three minutes. I'll bring some food. We're going out.'

'But the shop—'

'The shop doesn't matter.'

The shop had always mattered. Always.

'You're the one that matters, Nick. Not the shop.'

I stopped arguing. I went into the house and did as she said.

'Where are we going?' I asked when we were outside again.

'Anywhere,' she said over her shoulder. 'Anywhere we can talk. Come on.'

We climbed up on to the walls at Bloody Bank, the place where nearly eight hundred years earlier a man had been hanged for predicting the future and being wrong. We began to walk; we walked all the way round until the walls ended above the river. We stood there in silence for a long time, looking at the white masts seemingly growing out of the fields, and at the Purbeck Hills standing blue against the midday sky.

And after we'd eaten something and swallowed some hot coffee, we walked back again, much more slowly this time, until we came to the seat. And then we sat and talked.

Or Mum talked. I sat staring out over the countryside spread at our feet, and I listened. Because there was nothing else I could do.

'It wasn't any good, Nick. I knew that almost from the start. We ought never to have got married; we were so different. And he ... It was just as much my fault, I expect. Of course it was. But it wasn't any good.'

Her first husband. That's who she was talking about. John Watson.

'When you were born, I wanted to call you Nicholas. He didn't like the name; he said it was soppy. But I stood up to him for perhaps the only time in my life and I had it put first on your birth certificate. Nicholas John Watson. But he always called you Johnny, and after a time I did too. I thought it would muddle you up to have two different names.' She paused. 'He wanted you named after him, you see.'

'I see,' I said. From the corner of my eye I could see her hands twisting.

'Then, when things got bad, really bad ... when you were three ... I left. You and I left. And I came to Dorset and found a job where they let me live in and have you with me.'

'The Coulson Arms.'

'Yes.'

She'd been the cook. There'd been no Chef in those days; she did everything. She started work early every morning, did the breakfasts and the lunches; had the afternoons free, worked again in the evenings cooking meals. She and Johnny had had a room on the top floor of the hotel. During her working hours Johnny had played in the corner of the kitchen or, if it was fine, in the courtyard.

'The *courtyard*?'

'Yes.' Mum looked at me. 'The kitchen was in the centre of the building. It opened on to the courtyard.'

'Did it? It certainly doesn't now. It looks out at the side, near the lounge bar. You can see the sea from the bench outside. It's nowhere near the courtyard.'

'There were changes,' Mum said. 'Everything was changed afterwards.' She was looking down at her hands, remembering the past.

'Anyway,' she went on, 'you used to play in the

courtyard. The Rydals didn't mind. They never bothered about anything as long as the work was done. And I was a good cook, you know. They didn't want to lose me.'

'Yes,' I said. 'I'm sure.'

'I used to put your toys out on a rug and you'd spend hours out there, building things or cycling round on your little bike. The guests weren't in their rooms during the day so you didn't disturb anyone; you were always a quiet child. It was ideal. No traffic. It was so safe. That's what I thought.'

Safe? The courtyard? Then why was I filled with fear every time I thought about it?

I strained my memory for any trace of playing there happily, of being little Johnny Watson. There was nothing.

'After nearly a year there you were beginning to settle down, to forget – everything. It would all have been fine. Except for –' She stopped.

'Except for Sophie Rydal,' I said.

'So.' She smiled wryly. 'Jack Tillings has been busy. He always was an old gossip. I should never have let you take that job. I knew you'd meet someone who'd tell you everything.'

'Mum,' I said, 'I don't think he did tell me *everything*. All he said was he'd once worked there. And he mentioned Sophie Rydal. That's all.'

'Sophie,' she said. 'Everything went wrong because of Sophie ...'

Her voice died away. There was a long silence.

'Jack Tillings told me,' I said at last, 'that she was wild.'

'Oh, she could look as if butter wouldn't melt in her mouth,' Mum said, 'when she wanted to. Sometimes I'd see her in the mornings in her school uniform, setting off for the bus, and I couldn't believe it was the same child. But underneath she was always wild. Always.'

Like Jack Tillings, Mum blamed Sophie's parents.

'You couldn't really blame the child. Brian and Christine Rydal didn't mind what she did. They didn't seem to care, poor little kid. They were more interested in sitting drinking with customers till all hours. And meanwhile Sophie—'

'Yes?'

Mum's mouth tightened. 'She just did what she wanted. And we all had to put up with it.'

'That's what Jack said.'

But there was one way that Mum's account differed from Jack's. And that was his assertion that Johnny Watson had tagged along behind Sophie all day.

'No.' She shook her head. 'Really, I don't think it was like that. It was never like that. Sophie always took the lead. She wouldn't leave you alone.'

According to Mum, Sophie was always appearing in the kitchen offering to take Johnny off to play.

At the beginning it had seemed a good idea. 'A nice motherly ten-year-old to look after you. After all, you two were the only children living at the hotel. It could have been all right. Only, somehow, gradually I began to think that Sophie Rydal was not particularly nice or motherly.'

Sometimes they played together in the courtyard. Everything would go well for a while. Then there'd be trouble.

'I'd hear you cry. I'd go out, and a toy would be broken, or you'd have hurt yourself in some way.'

And Sophie would look at Mum with that sideways glance of her black eyes and say, 'Look what Johnny's done, Mrs Watson.'

119

Mum could never actually catch Sophie doing anything. It was simply that, whenever she was around, trouble soon followed.

'Now and again, perhaps when I'd been very busy for a while, I'd suddenly notice that everything had gone quiet outside. I'd go out into the courtyard, and realise the two of you had disappeared.'

'Disappeared?'

She nodded. 'There was a flight of steps under an archway leading up to the guest corridors. I'd always strictly forbidden either of you to go up there. But that's where I'd find you, playing in the corridors.'

'Yes,' I said. I couldn't remember it; only the dreams.

'Sophie liked to play hide and seek, racing round the corridors. The chambermaids told me. She'd hide, and have you running in and out of all the rooms that were unlocked, hunting for her.

'Once I came up and found you sobbing on your own. Sophie had hidden in a room that was going to be redecorated. Everything was draped in white dustsheets, and she'd hidden under one and jumped out at you, laughing and screeching. It scared you into fits.'

In my dreams, the white cloth hadn't been draped over furniture, but hung over a doorway. Dreams seem to be like that; they don't always get the details right. But most other things fitted. The voice, calling me. My fear of disobeying. And the face, laughing. To a four-year-old, a ten-year-old is a giant.

After the dustsheet incident, Mum had told the Rydals that she'd rather Sophie didn't play with Johnny any longer.

'It made no difference. Except that, after that, Sophie was angry. Angry with me – which didn't really

120

matter – but I think angry with you, too, because she thought you'd told tales. She grew more secretive, and began to get spiteful. She didn't ask any longer if she could play with you, but she went on doing it. She just made sure it was out of my sight.'

'In the garden, for instance,' I said slowly. 'On the lion.'

'Yes. She used to ride on it, with you sitting in front of her. I suppose Jack Tillings told you that.'

'Yes.'

It was true in a way. But Jack had talked only about Sophie riding the lion. He'd never mentioned Johnny riding too, squeezed in front of Sophie with her arms gripping him from behind, and being bumped up and down so hard on the stone saddle that he had cried.

I'd looked at that stone lion the first time I'd gone to the Coulson Arms for my interview, and a faint twinge of memory had stirred then, of myself on its back. And hating it. I had no other memories of the time when I'd been Johnny Watson at all – not even now. Only dreams.

Mum seemed to have stopped talking.

'And then, Mum?' I prompted. 'What happened then?'

'We left,' she said. 'That's all. Come on, Nick. We'd better go home now. Bring the flask, will you?'

I stood still. 'But –'

'Nick, I've told you all about it,' she said. 'We left the Coulson Arms. I came here, got a room for the two of us and looked for a new job. Dad was advertising for an assistant at the time, and I applied, and began working in the shop. My divorce was going through then. And when it was all cleared up, Dad and I got married. And Dad adopted you so that we could all be called Forester. A bit later, you started school, began

121

to make friends ... Then Daniel was born. And you forgot the past. We all did.

'You became Nicholas again. Nicholas Forester. We're all Foresters, Nick. We're a family. And if anyone remembers that we haven't always been – well, never mind. That's what we are. Johnny Watson belongs in the past. And so does Sophie Rydal. Leave them there. Please.'

I shook my head and went on standing there stubbornly.

'Oh, Nick!' she said, exasperated. 'If only it hadn't been the Coulson Arms where you found yourself a job. When you told us that evening, I didn't know what to say ... I tried to stop you ... I knew someone would start talking to you. Oh, why can't people let the past stay buried?'

'Because ...' Reluctantly, I began to follow her. 'Because it won't stay buried. It comes up again. It won't lie buried.'

And if you aren't allowed to know about it, I thought, it doesn't just crumble away. It stays deep inside you, buried, calling out to you in any way it can. In dreams, in my case. It must be listened to.

We walked along the top of the wall in silence until we reached Bloody Bank.

'Take the bag, Nick, while I get down, will you?'

I put out my hand to stop her.

'Wait a minute, Mum. There is something you haven't told me, isn't there? You haven't told me the whole truth. Something happened at the Coulson Arms, didn't it, that made you leave suddenly? Something bad?'

She gave a quick, unwilling nod.

'Something to do with Sophie Rydal?'

Another nod, her face turned away.

'And the courtyard?'

'Nick, leave it. Please. I don't want to remember it. And I don't want you to either. If you've forgotten, then that's the best thing that could have happened. It was horrible ... the police ... the reporters ... All of it.'

She looked at me pleadingly. 'It's over, darling. It was over long ago. The future's all that matters now.'

Chapter Eighteen

I lay on my back, under my duvet but still fully dressed, my arms straight at my sides, staring at the ceiling. The breeze from the open window was stirring the curtains and sending flickering shadows through the sunny room. The same sounds I'd heard all my life floated up from the street: the hoot and rumble of the traffic, slamming doors, voices hailing each other, the ping of the shop bell two floors below me.

Only I hadn't heard them all my life. Until I was four years old I hadn't even seen this town or this house. I'd lived in other places, other houses. I'd had a completely different life. And a completely different father.

'Don't worry about anything now, Nick,' my mother had said as she pulled on her overall and prepared to go back into the shop for the afternoon. 'You're completely worn out. Just go upstairs, darling, and have a good sleep. It'll all seem different after that, I promise you. Go along.' She gave me a gentle push towards the stairs. 'I'll pop up in an hour or so and make sure you're asleep.'

I went upstairs as she said and lay down. But I didn't sleep. Because inside me, like a vast solid block filling my chest, were all the things I'd been told that day. Told by Jack Tillings, told by his wife. Told by Mum herself.

I knew I mustn't touch the block, mustn't look at it, or even acknowledge that it existed. Because if I once did that, my whole life would split right open. I had to hold everything inside me very tightly together to stop that happening, at least for a few more hours. There was still one more thing I had to do. One last thing to find out.

What had happened at the Coulson Arms, that had been so dreadful that my mother had left abruptly and still couldn't bear to talk about it, eleven years later? What was it that bound Sophie Rydal and Johnny Watson and the courtyard together? What had turned Johnny Watson's safe, happy playground into the place of execution and terror I saw in my dreams?

I had to know. The time for hiding the truth had gone. Until I knew the whole story, every single part of it, I would have no peace. Everything now must be brought out into the light.

I pushed back the duvet, dislodging Quincey who'd been asleep on my feet.

'Oh, Quince, sorry.' She looked up at me resentfully. 'I forgot you were there.' I picked her up and buried my face in her soft neck, feeling the scalding tears threatening at the back of my chest. *Dad adopted you,* my mother had said. *Dad adopted you ...*

I swallowed hard. I mustn't think about it yet.

I gave Quincey one last hug and set her back on the bed in her warm hollow. I glanced at my watch. Twenty to three. There was still time to do it today. I went downstairs to the kitchen.

It had been Mum's mention of the police and reporters that had given me the idea. So, whatever had happened at the Coulson Arms eleven years before, had all been in the papers. I knew you could go to newspaper offices and read reports still kept on file years later; we'd done it once at school for a local history project. Perhaps I could find out that way. And, if so, I'd learn the truth at last, with nothing hidden from me.

I dug out the previous evening's paper and spread it on the table, rustling through the pages until I found the address of the office that published it. Then I went down to the shop.

For once it was empty of customers. Mum was listening to a sales rep. who was showing her boxes of chocolates for the Christmas trade.

'I'm going out for a while,' I said.

Dad looked up from the tray of jam tarts he'd been arranging. I knew Mum would have told him about our talk on the walls. They didn't have secrets from each other; only from me, I thought.

'Shouldn't you be resting, son?' he asked.

Don't, I cried inside. Don't call me that. I nodded, not looking at him. 'There's something I want to do,' I said.

'Well, then.' His forehead wrinkled anxiously. 'Let me take you in the car. Don't go on your own.'

'Thanks, but I need to go on my own. I'll be back before supper, I promise.' I went towards the door. 'Don't worry about me, I'll be all right.'

It took me three hours. At the end of that time, I knew. I knew, at last, everything there was to know.

On the train coming back from Weymouth, I sat opposite a young couple. He had spiky black hair and a silver earring. She had a purple miniskirt and green eye shadow. I forced all my concentration into trying to hear their conversation. Not because it was the least bit interesting but because, that way, I didn't have to think about what I had discovered.

It couldn't last. Soon, the couple got off and I was

126

left alone in the carriage, with the train speeding along through open country, not stopping any more. And then there was nothing else to think about but the newspaper stories that had been spread out in front of me at the office, and nothing else to see but the stark black headlines that I had been staring at.

PURBECK HOTEL HORROR ... DORSET
HOTEL GIRL'S TRAGIC GAME ...
The police said that, in their opinion ...
Medical evidence was given that ...
Miss Linda Beecham, hotel receptionist, said that ...
Mrs Joyce Watson, hotel cook, said that ...
Mr Brian Rydal, licensee of the Coulson Arms, said...
Mr Brian Rydal said that he and his wife Christine had been licensees at the Coulson Arms for eighteen months. On the day in question – 23 December – his daughter Sophie (10) had been at home, as the school holidays had just begun. After closing time at 2.30 p.m. he and his wife had remained in the lounge bar with several close friends as it had been their thirteenth wedding anniversary. He had also invited one or two members of staff to join them, among them Mrs Joyce Watson, the hotel cook, who was just going off duty for the afternoon. Mrs Watson's four-year-old son John and Sophie played together in the lounge bar. In answer to a question, Mr Rydal said that he considered his daughter to be a responsible child for her age. "The two children were good friends and often played together," he said ...

Bleak, formal words spoken in the hush of a coroner's court. I lay back in my seat as the train rattled towards home. Behind my closed eyelids, pictures were beginning to form themselves, pictures of the events of that winter's day eleven years earlier at the Coulson Arms Hotel.

No one now can tell exactly what any of the people involved actually said or thought. Especially thought. There are only the newspaper reports to go on and, for me, the things that the Tillings and Mum had told me too.

Other than that, to fit together what I think must have happened, I can only use my imagination.

Not my memory. However hard I strain to remember, I just can't. My memory doesn't touch any of it at all.

But I think it must have been something like this:

Once she'd finished the lunchtime food orders, Joyce Watson and her son Johnny always sat at the kitchen table and ate their own lunch. Then he cleared up his toys while she washed the floor. This done, she was free until her evening shift started at six.

As she walked through the lounge that day on their way up to their room, she saw a little crowd of people perched on high stools at the bar, laughing and smoking. That wasn't unusual. What was unusual was the fact that, as she went past, Brian Rydal put out his hand to detain her.

'Ah, Mrs Watson. Come and have a quick one.' He waved his glass at her. 'It's our anniversary. Thirteen years of the old ball and chain.' He winked at his companions. 'Lucky thirteen, eh?'

She knew he didn't like her, considered her standoffish. Especially since she'd told him she didn't want Sophie to play with Johnny any longer.

She smiled uncertainly. 'No, thank you, Mr Rydal.

I've rather a lot to do this afternoon.' She held Johnny's hand tighter.

'Oh, come on, Joyce.' Christine Rydal's words were friendly but her eyes were cool. 'Just one. It'll do you good.'

She perched unwillingly on the edge of a stool and accepted a drink. The room was strung with paper chains and Christmas lights. All round her, people were laughing and talking. The woman next to her offered her a cigarette but she shook her head. Several of the men were smoking fat cigars.

She looked over her shoulder for Johnny. Sophie was in a corner, punching the buttons on a machine of some kind, making it emit flashing symbols and whining sounds. Johnny was standing at a little distance, his hands clasped behind his back, staring up at her.

'Not finished yet?' Brian Rydal's voice boomed in her ear. 'Drink up, Mrs Watson. You've a long way to go to catch up the rest of us.'

Next time she looked round, the children were no longer there.

He'd never been able not to obey her. He knew his mother didn't want him to play with her and, deep down, he didn't want to either. But it was hopeless. She had a power over him that was absolute. Where she led, he always followed.

She could do anything. He followed her round the lounge as she flitted from one machine to another, lighting them up, making them play loud music or hurl brilliant pictures over the screen, even send money coursing out into her waiting hand, always keeping in the shadows.

Then she was out in the reception hall, beckoning

him. She ran across to the big staircase and beckoned again, giggling. The reception desk was empty; Linda Beecham was one of the people drinking at the bar. He toiled up the stairs, holding on to the banisters. Already, she was signalling to him from the corridors far above his head.

Down below, the laughing and talking went on.

She was waiting for him at the top. 'Hide and seek,' she said. 'Hide your face. No, properly, like this.'

She pulled him round to face the wall and pushed his forehead into the corner. 'Don't look. Don't you dare look until I call.'

Her footsteps pattered away, were lost. His knees trembled and he pressed them together. His eyes were screwed tight. This was almost the worst part. Not quite.

When she called, he set off down the corridor, looking fearfully from side to side. The doors on each side of him were closed. Everything was silent. The carpet was soft under his feet. No one knew he was there. No one would come and rescue him.

He hesitated outside a door, straining his ears. Was that her, laughing to herself inside?

He stretched out a hand and, inch by inch, turned the knob. Still holding it, he edged round the door and looked into the room.

It was half-dark, the curtains drawn. Everything was draped in white. As he stood staring, he saw to his horror a ghostly shape rise from the bed and swoop before him.

'No, NO.' She'd done this before; he couldn't bear it.

He was halfway down the corridor when she caught him.

'Baby!' She was laughing and tossing her black hair

back. The white cloth was draped round her shoulders. 'You're just a baby.'

She shrugged the cloth off on to the floor, losing interest. 'Come on, baby.' She gripped his arm. 'Hurry up.'

Stumbling, he tried to keep up as she swept him along the corridor. She flung a door open. At his feet, a flight of steps plunged down to vanish under a grey stone archway.

She said again, 'Come on.'

There was nothing to worry about, Joyce kept trying to reassure herself. The children must be somewhere in the building. Just playing, that was all.

'We'll be off in a minute.' The party in the bar had broken up a little before four. The Rydals had waved off their friends from the car park and were preparing to go out themselves, visiting more friends in Swanage. 'I'll just run up to the flat for the car keys,' Brian Rydal told Joyce.

'What about Sophie?' she asked.

He shrugged. 'Oh, she's probably up in the flat. We'll collect her on our way out, don't you worry.' His speech was slightly slurred. 'You worry too much, Mrs Watson. We'll all three be back by six, okay?'

She nodded. She had to find Johnny.

She went up to their room but he wasn't there. She crossed to the window and looked down. By leaning right out she could scan the whole courtyard. There was no one there. Sighing, she left the room and began to search the corridors.

It was an hour later that he came back.

By then, Joyce was frantic. She and Linda, the receptionist, had searched every bedroom, every bar and lounge for Johnny. She'd been right round the Rydals' garden, calling, and even run all down the village street, asking everyone she met if they'd seen a little boy in brown trousers and a brown and yellow jersey.

When, finally, she went back to the room, ready to ring the police, he was there. He was lying on the rug in front of the television, scribbling with his crayons on a sheet of paper.

'Johnny, where've you *been*?'

He had no explanation. He went on scribbling, occasionally glancing up at the screen where a red-robed choir was singing *Hark the Herald Angels Sing*.

'Where's Sophie?'

He shrugged.

'Johnny, I'm talking to you. Where is she?'

'Gone.' He put down a blue crayon and picked up a red one.

'Gone? Do you mean gone with her parents in the car?'

He nodded. The point snapped off the red crayon. Without lifting his eyes from the paper, he reached out for another one.

Is that how it was? Perhaps.

What is known for certain is that at five minutes to six, she and Johnny left the room again. On the way to the kitchen she bumped into Brian Rydal, red-faced, his fur collar turned up against the cold.

'Has Sophie behaved herself?' he asked.

She stared. 'Sophie went with you,' she said. 'To Swanage.'

'No, of course she didn't. I left her here in your charge.'

'Mr Rydal, you didn't. You said you – We haven't

seen her all afternoon. I'm sure she isn't in the building.'

She saw his face change. 'Then we'd better find her,' he said. 'Quickly.'

They called in the police at half-past seven, when they'd run out of places to look. The police carried out another, more systematic search throughout the hotel, looking in every room and corridor, every cupboard and cranny.

It was ten o'clock when they found her, and the stars were glittering in the frosty sky overhead.

Some weeks before, Brian Rydal had decided to replace some of the kitchen equipment. He'd turned two or three items out into the courtyard and bought new ones. The old ones had stayed in the courtyard, waiting for him to get round to taking them away. One of them was a large chest freezer.

When the police lifted the lid, they found Sophie inside. It was clear from the tests they did that she had been dead for several hours. The freezer was of an old-fashioned design that had no way of releasing the lid from the inside. From the condition of her hands they concluded that she had knocked and knocked to try to summon help.

The inquest verdict was Accidental Death.

I opened my eyes. The train had stopped at Wool Station. One or two carriage doors slammed, a few cars and bicycles waited at the level-crossing gates. Then a whistle blew and, with a jerk, the train started again. The next station would be mine.

But there was one last thing I still had to face, one more piece of evidence that was given at the inquest. Given by Brian Rydal. Of course. Joyce Watson would never have given it. Even thinking of it sent a chill through me, as it must have sent a chill through that court eleven years ago.

Brian Rydal confirmed that he had met Joyce Watson and Johnny at six o'clock when he had returned to the hotel. What she had not said, though, was that the place that they bumped into each other was the top of the steps leading down to the courtyard. And that Johnny Watson was refusing to go down into the courtyard and cross it to go into the kitchen. He was crying hysterically, and clinging to the iron handrail.

Why?

Even now I find it hard to think about. And I may be wrong. I hope to goodness I am.

After all, no one knows exactly what the two children did in that hour or so before Johnny was found safe in front of the television in Mrs Watson's room. They questioned him afterwards, of course, but he seems to have told them very little. So it can only be guesswork. But it was clear in the news reports what they thought happened.

And I have the dreams. They were as distorted and imperfect as dreams always are, but they began to make some sort of sense. And I couldn't stop the pictures forming in my mind ...

I see two children in the courtyard on another, earlier day. She looks all round to make sure no one is watching. Then she picks up the little boy, struggling, and puts him in the freezer. Shuts the lid. Sits on it, swinging her legs and laughing as he screams inside. Finally, almost reluctantly, she lifts him out.

Surely, that was where the idea came from?

It was such a good place for hide and seek. She crouches there in the near dark, holding the lid slightly open with one hand, helpless with giggles, as he hides his face at the top of the steps. Then she calls. And she hears his footsteps coming nearer ... nearer –

It would take only a little strength to slam the lid with both hands and run away.

He runs under the arch and up the steps to the corridors. And then he realises he's alone for the first time in his life. He can't remember which floor he's on, or which way to go to find the room he lives in. He just runs and runs, helplessly; round one corner, then another, then another. But he can't find the way out.

There are doors in long lines on each side of him. He flings one open, thinking it's their own door. But there are white cloths everywhere and he remembers her face, laughing at him. He retreats to the corridor and goes on running and he thinks he sees the way out. But there's a panel coming down in his mind, a lid, shutting out all the light, trapping him ...

When he finds the right room at last, his mother isn't there. He turns on the television; the sound of it blots out every other sound. He fetches his crayons and paper. Even when his mother comes back and questions him, he says nothing. He goes on crayoning, and listening to the television. He pushes down all the terrible thoughts deep, deep, where he thinks they can never come up again to trouble him.

In the darkening courtyard below the window, the knocking echoes round the grey walls and the empty kitchen. *Tap – tap – tap ... Tap – tap – tap ...*

Until it stops.

No one will ever know the truth. Not now.

When the train pulled into the station and I stood up to go, tiredness hit me in a huge wave. I stumbled along the platform and out of the station and turned towards home. The sun was low in the sky. People were strolling along, cycling past calling to each other, queuing in the chip shop. All of it was unreal to me; far, far away.

I didn't want to go home, but where else was there to go?

I walked across the back yard and pushed open the door. A warm cooking smell engulfed me. I turned my head away and started up the stairs.

'Nick?' Mum came out of the kitchen. 'You're just in time, darling. I'm doing cauliflower cheese.' Behind her I saw Dad and Daniel, sitting ready at the table.

'No, thanks,' I said. I went on up the stairs.

Mum followed. 'Some soup, then? Or I'll bring you up a hot drink.'

'No. I don't want anything. I'm going to bed.'

'But—'

I turned round. 'Look, Mum, I know.' I was so tired my tongue could scarcely shape the words. 'I've read it all. Everything.'

Mum didn't answer. I saw Dad in the kitchen doorway, and Daniel's puzzled, uncomprehending face. I felt utterly alien to them all.

'All I want is to go to bed. All right?'

I dragged myself up the last flight. I heard her say something and start to come up after me but by then I'd reached my room and closed the door.

Chapter Nineteen

There were only three days left until the beginning of term. As far as I possibly could, I spent them alone.

I avoided family meals by slipping into the kitchen when it was empty, and pocketing any food I could find. Then I'd creep out of the house and start walking. Anywhere. I walked for miles in those three days. Along the river bank, through country lanes, round and round the town walls, not noticing where I went or who I passed, not caring; simply trudging along with my eyes on the ground.

Only two thoughts churned endlessly in my head ...

I'm nobody. Oh, I'd thought I was. I'd thought I was Nick Forester, of Forester & Son. Only that was wrong, totally wrong. I wasn't a Forester. I wasn't even Nick. A person called Nicholas Forester had been invented when I was four years old. I'd been too young to protest when the name was pushed on to me. But it wasn't my name. I had no right to it. They'd let me live a lie for years and years. And they'd all known it was a lie except me.

If they took a family photograph now, it wouldn't be me leaning against Roger Forester's legs as the next '& Son'. It would be Daniel, his proper son. Not me. I wouldn't be in the picture at all. I was an outsider, an alien ...

And a murderer. That was the real me. Not Nick Forester, with his safe happy life with no problems in it. I was something else.

I was Johnny Watson. Johnny Watson who, before he was five years old, had deliberately and knowingly murdered someone. A life had been stopped, wiped out, because of me. Because of my bad blood.

That was it. I'd had bad blood in me from the beginning, handed on from my namesake, John Watson. He'd been a bad lot too, so bad Mum hadn't even told me about him properly. I couldn't remember him, had never even seen a picture of him, but his genes were in me and I knew whose son I truly was.

I was following in John Watson's footsteps, leaving a trail of blood behind me. Bad blood.

I walked until my feet were sore and my head throbbed with the thoughts going round and round. Then I turned for home. But unwillingly, because it wasn't home any longer.

I would walk into the house and up the stairs, and they'd call to me and try to ask me questions. Where had I been? Would I like supper? Wasn't there anything I would like? Please would I talk to them?

I couldn't. I could only shake my head and go on climbing the stairs and leave their questions and their anxious faces behind. The only thing I wanted was the attic room with its low sloping ceiling and its bed, where I could lie down and stare at that ceiling and go on thinking.

I'm nobody, I thought, hour after hour after hour. *I'm nobody ... and I'm a murderer.*

And Dad isn't my father.

'Why don't you come downstairs, Nick? Come on, darling. Dad and I want to talk to you.'

'What about?'

'We need to talk about it all. So that you understand—'

138

'There's no point. I understand it already.'

'But we can't bear to see you so unhappy. You are unhappy, Nick, aren't you?'

'Not particularly.'

It was fractionally better once school started again. The first morning of term, I found myself getting up and collecting my stuff and leaving the house at the right time, almost as if nothing had happened. It was a relief, in a way. There'd be a routine waiting for me at school, something to hold on to, something that might stop me sinking under the weight of the thoughts in my head.

Luckily, it was the start of a new school year. I was in the eleventh year now, suddenly very near the top of the school. All the teachers were reminding us that the exams would be on us in a few months and that we needed to get down to some serious work. And that was what I wanted. That first morning, I set my teeth and swore I'd bury myself in work.

Over the next few weeks, my grades and assessments slowly rose. 'Well done, Nick,' began to be written on pieces of work. 'Much better,' and 'You should do well if you keep this up.' At least the staff were pleased, anyway. I just wished *I* was.

'Your mother's just made some coffee, Nick. Why not come down and get warm? You can't work all the time, you know.'

'I thought you wanted me to work. Anyway, this has to be in tomorrow and it's nowhere near finished.'

'Let's have a look. I used to be quite good at maths once.'

'I don't think you'd understand it, actually. It's all changed since your day.'

There was an unbreakable barrier between me and everyone else. Wherever I went.

'Hey, Nick, sit here.' Cathy, hailing me across the dining hall. 'We haven't got the plague, you know.'

Reluctantly, I took my tray across. I unloaded it, sat down and took a book from my pocket.

'For goodness sake, Nick.' Cathy leaned over and flipped it shut. 'History! Do you have to? You haven't heard a word Alison's been saying to you.'

'Sorry.' I found my place again.

'What's got into you lately? Cycling past us in the mornings, sitting on your own in the library every spare minute ...'

'He's in training,' Phil observed. 'For the Superbrain of the Universe contest. We'll see him on the box any day now.'

Cathy shook my arm. 'Alison's only been telling you it's her birthday on Saturday. Only been inviting you to go skating in Bournemouth that evening with the rest of us. Only been –'

I lifted my head and met Alison's eyes, fixed on me from across the table. It was Alison who'd first told me about the S.A.N.D. disco, and from there I'd gone back to the Coulson Arms and found the courtyard.

I shook my head. 'Sorry,' I said. 'I'll be busy that evening. Excuse me.'

I picked up my plates and went to sit by myself at a corner table that had just become vacant. I began to eat without noticing what I ate, reading with fierce concentration to shut out the memory of Alison's hurt face. I only glanced up once, and that was when Phil went past on his way out and gave me a look that I interpreted as almost pure dislike. I bent my head and went back to my book.

The leaves turned brown and dropped on to the wet earth. My breath steamed now in the sharp air and my hands were cold on the handlebars as I cycled past Bloody Bank each morning on the way to school. The dreams had stopped, but now inside my head the thoughts churned and circled and twisted instead.

I'm nobody.

I'm a murderer.

Dad isn't my father.

'Nick, Mum says lunch is ready.'

'I don't want any.'

'Don't you? But it's Mum's special Sunday lunch. It's—'

'I'm not interested what it is. Go away. I'm working ...'

'... Nick, what's this Daniel tells me? Are you coming to eat with the rest of us or aren't you?'

'I'm too busy.'

'That's ridiculous. Listen, Nick, Dad and I understand you feel bad and we want to help you. But no one can help if you cut yourself off like this. So please, darling, come down and have lunch. Then we could sit and have a talk.'

'There's nothing to say.'

'There's a great deal to say. Look, don't keep treating me as though it was all my fault. I did my best—'

'Of course it was your fault. You took me to the Coulson Arms in the first place. You let it happen. And you've been lying to me ever since, you and Granny and ... and ...'

'Oh, Nick ...'

'Leave me alone. Don't touch me. And shut that door, please. It's draughty.'

'Oh, you're – Truly, Nick, I've had nearly as much of this as I can take. I don't think I can –'

'Can what? Live with me any more? Don't worry about that. I can always move out, you know. Get on a train to London, find myself a job. Plenty of people do that.'

'Nick, stop it. Do you think you're the only person in all this that's got any feelings?'

'I don't know what you mean.'

'No, and you're not trying to, are you?'

The rain dripped all day. In the evening, the church bells sounded through the gathering autumn dark. I stood at the window and watched the drops trickling down the glass and felt myself entirely empty with misery.

Two storeys down, the street door slammed. Daniel came out on to the pavement under the window, crossed the street and set off towards the church where he sang in the choir. His head was bent against the rain. I saw him take off his glasses and wipe them. He didn't look up.

The next day was Monday. Cross-country day.

The rain had stopped but the ground was squelchy soft. A cold blustery wind whipped round the school buildings as a little cluster of us set off at mid-morning and pounded in single file along the footpath bordering the school playing fields. Then, when we reached the end, we were able to space out and soon I'd settled down somewhere near the front, running at a good easy pace.

That's why I'd switched that term to cross-country running from rugby, which had been my major sport previously. With cross-country, I could be alone with

142

my thoughts; no one bothered me. I couldn't seem to take the close contact of rugby any more.

I scrambled over a stile already muddy with footprints and picked up my pace again on the far side, skirting a field of cabbages and making for an open gateway on the far side. I knew the route well; I'd done it several times that term already.

My breath puffed steadily in the chilly air. My feet had got soaked in the first few minutes but I was warm all over, keeping the two leaders in view but with plenty of space round me.

'Hey, Nick.' I hadn't heard Phil coming up behind me. 'Okay, mate? Mucky, isn't it?'

I grunted.

He kept pace with me as we went round the edge of the next field, bordering a little wood. A pigeon flew up from the leafless trees, its wings rattling sharply. Everything dripped with moisture.

'Are you okay, Nick? I never seem to see you lately.'

'I'm okay.'

The field plunged quite steeply ahead of us. I saw the two leaders reach the bottom and jump the little stream and go on up the far side.

'Guess what, Nick,' Phil went on. 'What do you think my dad did last night? He went out and —'

I stood still and faced him. 'Why don't you shut up, Phil? And save your breath for running?'

There was a second's silence.

'Sorry,' he said stiffly. 'Just trying to cheer you up.'

'Well, don't,' I said. 'I want to be on my own.'

'All right, then. Be on your own. Be like that.'

I turned away from him and ran on down the hill, leaving him standing there. The stream was scarcely wider than a ditch and I took it in one jump. But I hadn't reckoned on the churned-up slippery ground.

I fell sprawling on the far side, half in and half out of the icy water. I lay still for a minute. Then, gasping, I dragged myself up and staggered a few steps. I nearly fell again and had to cling to a tree trunk for support.

'I can't ...' I gripped the tree with both hands. 'I can't ...'

'Nick?' The voice seemed far away. 'Are you all right?'

'I can't ... I can't ... I can't ... I can't ...'

'Nick?' Running steps coming nearer. 'What is it? Are you hurt?'

I clung tighter to the tree. 'I can't bear it ... any of it.' The words burst from me in spurts. 'I didn't mean to be so horrible ... I can't stop saying such horrible things all the time ... I don't mean to –'

'Nick, it's Phil. What's the matter?' He tried to prise my fingers from the tree. 'What is it?'

'I've got to talk to somebody ... Somebody listen ... Listen, please ... Please listen –'

'I'm listening. But I can't hear you very well.'

With an enormous effort I turned round. I saw Phil's frightened face staring at me.

And it was only then I realised I was crying, great sobs that tore from my chest, from so deep inside me they were shaking my whole body. There seemed to be nothing at all I could do to stop them.

It was Phil who got me back.

'He'll be okay,' he kept saying, steering me firmly back up the field through the little knot of runners who'd caught us up by then. 'Leave him alone. I'll see to him.' His arm was round my shoulders, holding me up. 'He's just hurt himself somehow. That's all.'

But that wasn't all. It was nothing like all. I knew that.

Even while I was being helped back to school, and then being examined in the sickroom and, later, waiting for Dad to come and take me home, I knew what really was wrong with me.

It wasn't any physical injury. I'd twisted my ankle slightly, and I was soaking wet and a bit bruised, but it wasn't that which kept the tears flowing down my face in an unstoppable stream, and wrenched the sobs out of me. It was something quite different.

I lay in bed at home that evening, trying to drink the hot milk that Mum was anxiously offering me, trying to tell the doctor what was the matter, trying to find any words for what ailed me, and all the time, deep inside me, I knew what was causing it all.

It was grief.

I was crying for Sophie Rydal, who'd died alone in terror in the dark; and for Johnny Watson, who'd only been four years old. Crying for Daniel, who I'd taken for granted was my little brother. For Mum, who'd had to hear me say that everything that had happened was her fault. And for Dad, who wasn't my dad at all.

And I cried for myself, too, because I didn't know who I was, whether I was Johnny Watson or Nicholas Forester or just a nobody person who had no proper name and didn't belong anywhere.

I cried and cried and cried, until there were no more tears anywhere to cry. And then I slept.

Chapter Twenty

I spent a large part of the next week asleep. Deeply asleep, too deep for any dreams, making up at last for the months of disturbed nights and all the tension.

Some mornings, I'd try to get up and dress and go to school. But my legs seemed too weak to hold me up.

'Could be a touch of this virus going round,' the doctor said. 'That, and pushing yourself too hard at school. Take it easy for a week or two.'

So I did. I lay back on my pillows and watched the world going past below the window, with Quincey purring on the sill and my radio and tapes by the bed to keep me company. Down below, the shop bell pinged as customers went in and out. Mum and Dad had brought their summer assistant back so that they'd have more time to spend with me. They even talked of keeping her on permanently so that each of them could take a half-day off each week.

There was time to think. And to talk.

'Everyone's dead envious of you, mate.' Phil perched on the end of my bed one afternoon after school, peeling me a satsuma. 'Lolling round here at home while the rest of us are getting our gruesome mock-exam results back. Incidentally, you seem to have done your usual brilliant stuff in the mocks before you swooned away.'

I took the satsuma and split it into segments. 'What do people think's wrong with me?' I asked.

'Oh, I told them you broke both legs on the cross-country.'

'You didn't! I'll have them all round here trying to write rude things on my plaster casts.'

'I'll say you've got something more internal, then. Internal fractures.'

Internal fractures. It sounded quite a good description of what had happened to me.

'I've got loads of messages for you, if I could only remember them,' he said. 'Oh, yes. Alison sends her undying love to you, or something like that –'

'Phil, you're kidding. *Alison?*'

'Of course.' He reached over and took the last two segments of fruit. 'Haven't you ever noticed? You go round with your eyes shut, that's your trouble.'

I lay there, thinking about it. I needed to talk to Alison anyway, about the sponsorship money I'd forfeited by leaving the S.A.N.D. disco before the end. Perhaps there was some way I could raise the money myself and pay it in. Maybe at the same time I'd ask if she'd go skating with me one evening. The only problem was I couldn't skate. But maybe she'd teach me ...

'I'll see you, Nick.' Phil heaved himself to his feet. 'In a day or two. I just wanted to check you were okay.'

'Oh, yes. Just tired, that's all.' There'd been a questioning note in his voice. Perhaps I'd tell him some of the story one day. Not yet. There were other people I had to talk to first.

Later, Mum came up to sit with me.

'What's that you've got there, Nick?'

'Oh, I just thought I'd have another look at them.'

I'd fetched the family photograph from the landing and propped it up on my bedside table where I could study it. Great-grandfather, Grandfather,

Grandmother, Roger Forester and his three sisters, all looked steadily back at me.

'It's funny, you know,' I said. 'I always thought I looked like them. Especially Dad. I mean – people used to say it, didn't they?'

She nodded. 'Often. It was funny, really. But you are like them, in a way. Same squarish face, dark hair. Quite different from me.'

'Or Dan.'

'Yes.'

There was a long silence.

'I wish you'd told me,' I said at last. 'That's one of the things that's so awful. Everyone knowing all the time. Except me.'

'Not everyone,' she corrected quickly. 'Only Dad and me.'

'And Granny. She must have known. Well, obviously. But she never gave me a clue I'd once been ... different. Not even when I was with her this year. She could have said –'

'I asked her not to,' Mum said. 'She was always doubtful. But I thought you could forget and start a new life. And I did –'

'Did what?'

'Did try to talk to you at first. When you were little. About your real father, about the Coulson Arms and what happened to Sophie. But you didn't let me. You got dreadfully upset every time. I couldn't bear it. So in the end, I let it go. But I did try.'

'You should have done.' I turned away from her. 'It wasn't fair.'

'Perhaps not.' She spoke in a small voice. 'Nick, I'm sorry if I made the wrong decision. Sometimes parents have to make hard choices and they get them wrong. If I did, I'm sorry.'

'It's okay. Don't worry.' I felt as if she was a stranger. 'Did she come to the wedding?'

'Wedding? Who?'

'Granny. To your first wedding.'

'Well ... yes. Yes, of course. I've got some pictures of it if you'd—'

'No,' I said. 'I don't want to see them. Thanks all the same.'

After a day or two, I began to get up and move around the house. I watched TV, made tea at intervals and took it through to the shop, played games with Daniel when he was at home.

'This is good,' he remarked, dealing out another hand for a card game he was trying to teach me. 'You being home, not doing any work.'

'Oh, that's okay,' I said. 'Just so long as it suits you.'

'I didn't mean that. I know you've been upset or something. Dad and Mum told me.'

'Did they? What did they say exactly?'

'Oh,' he said vaguely. 'About you once having had a different father or something. About Mum being married to someone else.'

'Yes?'

'I think that was it,' he said. 'Something like that. But Mum's married to Dad now, isn't she, and he's our father, so what's all the fuss about?'

'Well ...' I said. Then I picked up my cards.

'Come on, Dan, let's play. This time, I'm really going to get the hang of it.'

Three days later, the doctor said I was well enough to go back to school next day if I felt up to it. There were still two weeks of term to go before Christmas.

That afternoon, I wandered restlessly around the

house and eventually down to the shop. Dad was in the little room at the back, going through some invoices, while Mum and their assistant, Ann, coped with the customers.

'What are you going to do on your last afternoon before school, Nick?' Mum asked.

'I don't know. Maybe I'll go for a walk or something.' Somehow, I'd lost the taste for solitary walking since I'd been in bed. 'I can't ask anyone to go with me. They're all in school.'

Dad looked up. 'What about a ride out to the coast or somewhere? It'd do you good, if you wrap up well.'

'You'd never guess it, Nick,' Mum put it, 'but this is supposed to be Dad's first half-day. His idea of time off is to sit there and come running to serve every time the door opens. Take him out from under our feet, do.'

A cold north-easterly wind was blowing, and an occasional tiny speck of snow fluttered like dust past the windscreen as we drove down to Swanage.

'I'm not sure this is a good idea,' Dad said, as he locked up the car near the sea front and glanced at the heavy grey sky. 'After you've been indoors so long—'

I shook my head. 'It's great. Exactly what I need.' I took a big breath of sharp air. 'It's good to be out of doors again.'

The shops were full of Christmas lights and glitter. We wandered along the main street looking in windows, and then turned up the hill towards the headland and the coast path.

'Are you sure you're warm enough, Nick?'

'Fine. Not cold at all.'

We climbed up to Peveril Point and stood together at the top, looking back over Swanage Bay. The sea was very calm; the waves turning over gently. Beyond the town, the tall white chalk stacks known as Old Harry Rocks stood out at sea, with sea birds circling their grassy tops.

Dad took his binoculars from his pocket. 'Guillemots.' He passed them to me. 'Take a look.'

We began to walk along the coast path to Durlston Head.

'All right for school tomorrow?' Dad asked.

'I don't know. There'll be a terrible lot of catching up to do.'

'I think you'll be all right,' Dad said. 'Look how you worked at the beginning of term. Most youngsters would have gone to pieces when they'd found out what you found out. They'd have started truanting or gone on drugs or something. You were always a very steady lad.'

I managed a watery smile. 'Was I?'

'Always. Right from the start.'

A haze was closing in over the sea. The daylight was not going to last much longer. In unspoken agreement we turned back.

'I must –' I licked my lips and tried again. 'I must be like ... John Watson. You know ...' It was the first time I'd said his name to anyone.

Dad stood still on the path.

'You could be, I suppose,' he said. 'But with not seeing him for so many years, I shouldn't think you are very much. There are other people you're more likely to take after.'

'Who?'

'Well.' He considered. 'There's your mother and me, to start with. You've lived with us for as long as you can remember. That must count for something.'

'Maybe.'

'People often remark how you're like me, you know.

That's how you get, living together. You grow together.'

I nodded unwillingly. Down in the little town, the lights were coming on all round the bay.

'You know,' Dad went on after a moment, 'it took me a bit of time to get used to it all. I mean – it wasn't just that I got married. I had a ready-made son at the same time. I had a son suddenly who was four years old. It took time.'

I looked at him. 'Did it?'

He smiled. 'Oh, yes. But I reckon I managed it. Hope so.'

Perhaps I'd have to learn to be his son too, all over again. Differently.

'I – I keep thinking about him,' I burst out. 'John Watson.' I couldn't say 'my father' somehow. It would sound wrong. 'Maybe he'll turn up one day and sort of – you know – claim me. Take me back.'

'Is that what you'd like?'

'No.' I didn't have to think about it. 'I'd hate it.'

'Lots of people would like it,' Dad said. 'We're not all the same. But no one can make you do anything you don't want to. Anyway, he's never come yet. We wouldn't be hard to find. But he made a new life for himself. Got a new wife ...'

I looked up. 'Did he?' A load slipped from my mind. 'Are you sure?'

'Certain. That's why he wanted the divorce.'

We began walking again. After a while he said,

'You can always find out more about him, you know, if you want to. Your mother – well, she finds it hard to talk about it all – but I'm sure she would if you asked her. You have a right to know.'

'I don't want to know.'

'All right,' Dad said. 'You can always change your

mind. Now, how about a cup of tea in the town before we go back? I mustn't be away from the shop for too long.'

It snowed that weekend, and that gave everyone something different to think about. Phil and I went ploughing all along the river path, kicking up the smooth whiteness like a couple of kids. On our way home we passed the supermarket and saw a board outside, offering jobs for the Christmas holiday.

'Going to have a go?' Phil looked at me.

'Why not?'

'Just as long as you don't bring your textbooks to work with you every day.'

'No chance.'

In fact, I was taking the doctor's advice and not pushing myself too hard for these last two weeks. I'd catch up eventually. Dad was right; things took time.

'Come on, then,' said Phil.

I stood still, eyeing him. 'Are you serious? They'll never give you a job dressed like that.'

But they did. They took us both on and we started work the day after school broke up. It solved my problem about the sponsorship money. And it was quite good, working with Phil again.

One evening, walking home from work, I found myself almost tempted to tell him the whole story of Johnny Watson and Sophie Rydal. Almost.

We were good friends, Phil and I. Always had been and probably always would be. But nobody's good at everything. Phil was good at making people laugh and making life interesting. You couldn't expect him to listen to stories and keep them to himself as well as all that. That would be pushing things too far. It didn't make any difference to Phil and me being friends.

Chapter Twenty-one

I came to the top of the last hill and stopped to get my breath back. The village was spread out below me. It seemed bigger than it had in the summer, probably because the trees were bare now and the gardens almost empty. Thin curls of smoke rose from many of the chimneys of the thatched cottages. In the distance, the sea gleamed in the pale winter sun.

I cycled on down the hill and past the Coulson Arms – not looking at it – and came to a halt outside the small grey-towered church next door. Leaving my bike against the railings, I climbed the shallow steps and found myself in the churchyard.

It was quite a small plot of grass around the church, bumpy and uneven with age and much digging. Some of the gravestones leaned over at angles; others were so encrusted with golden lichen that their inscriptions were unreadable. But the new graves were neat and well-cared-for. Many had flowers on them or Christmas wreaths of holly and fir cones and red ribbon.

It was only a hunch I had. Just an idea. But a strong one nevertheless.

I found the grave in a corner of the churchyard, just the other side of the hedge that separated the church from the Coulson Arms' path that led to Mr Briggs's garden. I must have been within touching distance of it that first day when I came for the interview; the day I saw the stone lion.

The words on the headstone were brief:

SOPHIE RYDAL

Dearly Beloved Daughter of Brian and Christine

Aged 10 years

That was all except for the date of her death. December 23. Exactly eleven years ago. And the words: *Safe in the Arms of Jesus.*

There were no flowers on it, no Christmas wreath. I went away rather quickly and walked down the village street. It was Sunday, but perhaps the shop would be open.

I discovered it crowded with last-minute Christmas shoppers. I spotted some bowls of blue hyacinths, ready wrapped in Christmas gift paper, and picked out the best one I could see.

Back in the churchyard, I placed the bowl rather awkwardly on the ledge in front of the headstone. I hoped it would rain soon and keep the bulbs fresh. I wondered if Sophie's parents, Brian and Christine, were remembering the date today, wherever they were now. And I thought about Sophie Rydal, aged ten, safe in the arms of Jesus.

She'd been dead for eleven years. If she'd lived, she'd have been twenty-one now.

Who had I really seen? On that bus ... In the classroom ... On the lion ... Standing at the window?

A ghost? The ghost of ten-year-old Sophie Rydal?

I wasn't the sort of person who saw ghosts.

All I knew was that, once, she'd been alive. She'd travelled on that school bus, she'd worn that purple T-shirt, she'd laughed as she'd ridden the lion. Once.

And that summer, I'd seen her. Just occasionally,

fleetingly. And eleven years late. I'd seen her. That was all I knew.

There's something in the Bible, isn't there, about seeing things 'through a glass darkly'?

Seeing her had been like that. Often it had been literally through glass that I'd glimpsed her; always distant, always quickly gone again. But there.

And the dreams, too, had been nothing more than fragments of the truth, and distorted fragments sometimes. All of it through a glass darkly.

But now I'd been brought face to face with the truth about myself. The dreams hadn't been a warning about the future, like a prophecy by Peter de Pomfret or something your horoscope says. They were about the past. My past, that I'd hidden from myself for so long. I'd been hiding from it ever since I'd turned on the television when I was four years old, so that I wouldn't have to think about Sophie downstairs in the courtyard.

Why had I never wondered how long my parents had been married, or asked them why there were no photographs of Dad with me as a baby? Perhaps I just hadn't thought of asking them. Or perhaps I didn't ask them because I hadn't wanted to know the answers.

Suddenly I remembered something. I remembered Mum standing on the Quay at home, talking to someone.

It had been sometime before Easter. I knew that because Mum and Dad had been busy selling Easter eggs in the shop. Then Mum had taken me across town to buy me some new shoes. And on the way home, she'd stopped to talk to this woman she'd met on the Quay.

Mrs Tillings. Jack Tillings's wife. That's who it had been.

She and Mum had bumped into each other on the Quay, years after they'd first known each other at the Coulson Arms, and I'd been standing there when it happened. How could I have forgotten that?

I'd shut it out, switched off, pretended it hadn't happened. Because Mrs Tillings was someone whose face I knew from the past, from the dark past I was determined not to remember. So my mind had refused to see her.

Soon after that, the dreams had begun. They'd been the last desperate attempt of my mind to make me remember. And a few weeks later I'd gone to Daniel's school to take him to the dentist, and I'd seen a girl looking at me through a bus window ...

I went to sit on a bench near the hedge and contemplated Sophie's grave. *Dearly Beloved*. I hoped she had been. So few people seemed to have loved Sophie Rydal. So many people made irritated and angry and afraid. There must have been another side to her, something different, if only you'd got to know her well enough. And now I'd never have the chance. Because she was dead. Because of what Johnny Watson had done.

Might have done, I reminded myself. Only might have done. They hadn't been sure at the inquest. Sophie might have closed the lid herself by mistake. Or it might have fallen shut on its own. Johnny Watson might not have had anything to do with it at all.

But he might have done. Almost certainly he did.

If only I could remember.

I'm sorry. I said it soundlessly. *I'm sorry. I didn't know. I was only four ...*

I wasn't ever going to know for certain. It wasn't that

easy. All I could do was learn to live with the uncertainty.

I sighed and looked up at the church clock. Nearly quarter to three. I'd have to go home soon. I'd told Mum and Dad I was going out, though not where I was going. This was one journey I had had to make alone.

'Nick?'

I jumped and looked round. The voice had come from the other side of the hedge.

'It's Nick, isn't it? Nick Forester?'

'Kirsty.' I stood up. 'How are you, Kirsty?'

'I'm fine. What you doing there?'

'Oh, just sitting.'

I went to the gate to meet her.

'Well.' She studied me, smiling. 'Still growing, I see. Have you missed us all?'

'Yes. I have.'

We strolled across the Coulson Arms' car park.

'Come and have a drink,' she said. 'I'm just going off duty.'

We sat by the log fire in the lounge bar and sipped tomato juice.

'Everything's changing,' Kirsty said. 'Mr Briggs has sold up to a business consortium. They were here that day you left – do you remember? It's going to be turned into a luxury conference centre. They'll add more rooms, build a squash court where the old courtyard is now ... You won't recognise it.'

'No,' I said. 'I suppose not.'

'Jeff and I are leaving after Christmas. We're going to work in a hotel in Spain.'

'Great.'

The winter afternoon was gathering in as I left. Granny

was arriving for Christmas on the coach from Plymouth at six. I ought to be home in good time to meet her.

'Take care, Nick.'

'And you. Bye, Kirsty.'

I collected my bike and checked the lights.

I took one last look at the Coulson Arms, and at the huddled village beyond. You couldn't see the sea any longer because the mist had closed over it.

Then I turned away, and began to push my bicycle up the long hill towards home.

Also by Frances Usher

MAYBREAK

One weekend in May never to be forgotten . . .

Mark, the best truant at Sapling Lodge, is going to meet his father even if everyone has said he has to stay in school . . .

Eric has to escape too, to find the house in Birmingham, or the bullies will take their revenge . . .

And Alex, Judith and Dorcas from the girls' boarding school next door all have something to prove . . .

Their lives become inextricably linked that extraordinary Bank Holiday weekend.

Vivien Alcock

A KIND OF THIEF

'Someone's got to look after the three of us.'

Elinor has always been seen as the strong one of the
family. When her father is arrested, her step-
mother can't cope and thirteen-year-old Elinor is
left to look after the family. But at the time of his
arrest, Elinor's father gives her the means to
retrieve his case – which Elinor believes must be
full of money.

Then, the children are sent off to different homes.
Elinor takes the case with her but Timon, who also
lives in Elinor's new home, makes her realise that
she too is a kind of thief . . .

'Convincing storytelling rich with atmospheric
imagery . . .'
The Guardian

Anne Fine

THE STONE MENAGERIE

Every Sunday Ally goes with his parents to visit his shadow-like Auntie Chloe in a mental hospital. Every Sunday Ally gets angry, thinking the visits a total waste of time. Until, one day, he sees the girl who has planted her own name in the mysterious, tangly land on the other side of the lake . . .

Anne Fine, winner of the Smarties Prize for *Bill's New Frock* and the Guardian Fiction Prize and Carnegie Medal for *Goggle-Eyes*, is much praised for her wit, ingenuity and 'sense of depth under playful surfaces, a light touch which can reveal the poignancy in the happiest relationship.'

'This is another excellent novel from a remarkable writer.'
Peter Hollindale, *British Book News*

Maeve Henry

A GIFT FOR A GIFT

Since her father left, things at home are impossible
for Fran. Her mother has given up trying to keep
the family together and Fran is left to look after the
house and her two younger brothers.

One night, in despair and anger, Fran storms out
of the house and seeks refuge in what seems to be
an empty house. But there she meets the strange
and elusive Michael, who has the power to grant
her any wish but who, in return, insists on a gift of
his own choosing – that Fran will stay with him in
this life and beyond.

A strong and beautifully written story of despair,
hope and self-realisation.

Garry Kilworth

THE DROWNERS

'Always treat a river with respect,' John Timbrell told each of his many children, when they reached an age of understanding. 'Never take her for granted. She don't strike often, but when she do, it's quick as an adder. River's got no concerns for age nor whether you be a boy or a girl. It'll take what's there, and never a thank'ee left behind.'

Tom Timbrell heeds his father's warning but still the river takes him – and with him goes the knowledge of the drowning of the fields which the local farmers rely upon for the successful tending of their land.

For two years the farmers struggle hopelessly until, one day, a mysterious young boy appears and begins to teach Jem Blunden the ways of the river, a boy whose age remains untouched by the passing of the years and who bears a remarkable resemblance to Tom Timbrell . . .

'A fine, exciting story, beautifully told.'
Leon Garfield

Shortlisted for the Carnegie Medal.

Catherine Sefton

THE SLEEPERS ON THE HILL

I wasn't afraid . . . not really afraid . . .

It was young Tom Connor who discovered the strange bangle and its owner, Kate, who was even stranger. Kate wouldn't say where the bangle came from, but Tom had his suspicions – and they increased as more and more trouble came upon the people of Ten Cottages. None of the local villagers would have dared to climb Sleepers' Hill, let alone take anything from the ancient graves beneath . . .

Cara Lockhart Smith

PARCHMENT HOUSE

From the outside Parchment House looks like any other house. But, home for the orphans of Carstairs and Bungho, it holds dark and sinister secrets. And, like the other orphans in the house, Johnnie Rattle is all alone in the world . . .

Governed by the worthies, the children live a life of drudgery maintaining the gadgets designed to make their superiors more comfortable. But when the 'ultimate' gadget arrives, life at Parchment House becomes intolerable. Archibald, a huge and gleaming robot, is programmed to control, discipline and educate the children. But when Archie's cruelty becomes too much for the orphans, Johnnie Rattle has the courage to instigate a rebellion. He risks everything to save the children . . .

In *Parchment House*, her first novel, Cara Lockhart Smith has created a nightmare world where good triumphs over evil. It is a wonderfully funny, original and touching fantasy.